A FATHER OF THE FATHERLESS

Brandon Kuperus

This book is a gift to you from your grade 6 teacher. I hope you had a great year, and I wish you God's blessing in the future.

Miss Oudshoorn

A FATHER OF THE FATHERLESS

Sjanie VanDuinen

Illustrations by Rino Visser

EARLY FOUNDATIONS PUBLISHERS

"A father of the fatherless..."
Psalm 68:5
Holy Bible
King James Version

This English edition is exclusively distributed by:
Early Foundations Publishers
3130 Vanderbilt Avenue
Portage, MI 49024-6062
U.S.A.
www.efpublishers.org

Originally published in the Dutch language as:
"Een Vader der wezen," by Sj. van Duinen.
Illustrations: Rino Visser
Originally published by J. P. van den Tol – © 1975 Dordrecht,
The Netherlands
3rd Edition – © 1982 Den Hertog B.V. – Houten,
The Netherlands

Translation: Marinus VanBrugge

ISBN 978-0-9742131-8-7

Printed in the USA by Color House Graphics, Inc.

Table of Contents

CHAPTER 1

"See you tomorrow, Lydia!"

"Okay, see you tomorrow. Bye!"

As Nellie and Robbie boarded the bus, they turned and waved once more to Lydia. She waved back and watched as the bus drove off, then slowly walked down the busy shop-lined street. Since she lived only five minutes away from school, it didn't take her long to get home, and Lydia wasn't in any hurry. Her friend, Nellie, had a thirty-five-minute bus ride before she got home.

Nellie's family was so nice. Her mother was cheerful, and her father was a lot of fun, too. He could be strict, but he also liked to tease and laugh with the children. Nellie's brother, Robbie, was a naughty seven-year-old boy, and Elise was the baby of the family.

If Lydia had a nice family, then she wouldn't mind living close to school. She would hurry home, excited to see her little sister and eager to tell her mother everything that had happened at school that day. But she did not have such a family, and Lydia found herself wishing she had to ride the bus so she could get home late, too.

As she left the busy shopping area, Lydia came to a quieter road and followed it to the end, where she turned left onto her own narrow street. All the houses on the street were old, and most of the people who lived in them were old, too.

Walking down her street depressed Lydia. She couldn't find anything cheerful about this neighborhood, even on sunny summer days. She wondered why anyone would want to live here. If she had a choice, she would move, but she had no choice and would have to stay here whether she liked it or not.

Near the end of the street, she stopped at house number 48 and rang the doorbell. As usual, she had to wait a little while before there was a response. Then she heard shuffling feet, the door opened a crack, and a shrill voice said, "Oh, it's you! You're late!"

Lydia entered the dark, narrow hallway and took off her coat and shoes. Inside, she found things as they usually were. Aunt Kate, who had opened the front door for her, was already busy in the kitchen again, while Aunt Trudy sat next to the potbelly stove dozing, with her knitting needles on her lap. She looked up for a moment when Lydia entered the room and mumbled, "Well…," before nodding off again.

Lydia sat down at the table by the window and stared outside. There was nothing to see but a little stone patio, a high wooden fence, and the neighbors' housetops behind them. Everything was dull and monotonous.

She drummed her fingers on the serving tray lying on the table, but at once Aunt Kate's shrill voice sounded from the kitchen, "Stop that drumming! You're making me nervous!" Lydia sighed deeply and thought, "I can hardly move around here. No matter what I do, it makes my aunts upset!"

Suddenly she remembered she had to study for tomorrow's history test. Now at least she had something to do.

******

That night, Lydia lay in her bed unable to fall asleep. Moonlight shone through the small attic window as she snuggled under the blankets, shivering a little from the cold. Determined to fall asleep, she closed her eyes tightly and tried counting to one hundred.

She had almost reached twenty when she stopped. “How silly! It wasn’t working at all.” She tried turning over to get more comfortable, but that didn’t help either; she was still wide awake.

She wondered why, because she usually didn’t have any trouble falling asleep. Deep down Lydia knew why. She had gone to bed angry that night, angry at everything and everyone, and now she was trying to ignore that little voice that said, “You didn’t pray.”

She had decided that she was not going to pray anymore. She figured it didn’t make a difference anyway. She had asked the Lord many times if He would change her aunts, because weren’t all things possible with the Lord? But it hadn’t helped. Both aunts remained the same, or, if anything, they seemed to be getting worse. Last night at suppertime was a good example of that.

Lydia had told her aunts that she would be home a little late the next afternoon. Her teacher wanted them to practice for the Christmas program they were going to have at school Friday afternoon before Christmas vacation.

Before Lydia finished, she regretted saying anything, because Aunt Kate’s face became fiery red, and she yelled, “Christmas program? Christmas program! You might as well forget that! They are brainwashing you at that Christian school. Foolish child! You believe everything they tell you there. I’m going to pull you out of that school and send you to a public school, even if it means you have to take the bus. You have cost me enough money already, so a little more bus fare won’t make much difference.” She went on and on.

Lydia still shivered when she thought about all the nasty comments Aunt Kate had made during her tirade. Aunt Trudy, as usual, hadn't said a word but had just nodded her head in agreement. Lydia didn't say anything else either, and right after supper Lydia had been sent upstairs to her room.

Usually she felt sad when her aunt raved like that, but this time she was angry. All her dreams of being in the Christmas program had vanished. She also knew Aunt Kate wouldn't waste any time pulling her out of her school, away from the school where Bible stories were read every morning, and away from her only friend, Nellie.

Going to that school was the only thing she enjoyed. Now it would all be over, and there would be nothing left to look forward to. She would have to go to a strange school with children she didn't know. She would never be able to hear Bible stories again, and she wouldn't have a teacher who prayed anymore, either. Everything would be different.

Lydia couldn't bear the thought of such a change, but she knew she didn't have any choice. Ten-year-old girls don't get to make those decisions. Whatever her aunts decided would be final.

Thinking about all of this had made Lydia angry, and that's why she had decided to stop praying. She started thinking that maybe Aunt Kate was right after all. Maybe everything written in the Bible wasn't completely true.

And yet, she enjoyed it so much when stories about the Lord Jesus were told at school. They reminded her of Papa's letter which he had written to her when he was very sick and knew he was going to die. Her mother had already died when the letter was written, and Lydia was just a little baby, a sweet, cheerful little girl who didn't know that she would soon be an orphan, without a father or mother.

Since her aunts never talked about them, Lydia knew very little about her father and mother. She knew that they had been famous performers in the circus, and that a very bad accident had happened, but exactly what had happened, she didn't know.

She had the letter from her father, though, and she wouldn't give it up for a million dollars. Even though she didn't understand everything he had written and she had no one to explain to her what her father actually meant, he wrote much about the Lord Jesus, and that made her very happy.

Now Lydia was angry, and she didn't want to think about the letter anymore! What good would it do her? The letter couldn't help her either, she thought angrily.

How she wished her parents were still alive. Everything would have been so different.

Father had written that it all had to be this way, because while they were working at the circus, they hadn't believed in God. He had warned her in the letter that when she became older, she should never go to the circus because there the Lord was not feared, and His Name was mocked.

Without realizing it, Lydia was thinking about that letter again.

There was one sentence in it that was especially dear to her: "My dear child, whatever happens in your life, tell the Lord about it. He is a Father of the fatherless." She cried again when she thought about those words. Then she jumped out of bed, knelt down beside it, and prayed, "Lord, Thou art able to help me. I am so lonely, and I do not want to go to a different school. Wilt Thou please forgive everything? For Jesus' sake. Amen."

Quickly she crawled back under the blankets. Her anger was gone now, but she still felt sad and very lonely. She pressed her face deep into the pillow and softly continued crying.

The moonlight shone on the sorrowful little girl, but the moon couldn't help or comfort her! Nevertheless, higher, much higher than the moon, the Lord lives. He hears the prayers of sad little children, and He is able to help!

CHAPTER 2

"It's nice and sunny out today, isn't it, Nellie?" Lydia asked.

"It sure is!" Nellie replied.

The two girls walked past the playground to the bus stop, where Robbie was waiting for them.

School had been let out fifteen minutes early because of Christmas vacation. The girls had stayed to help the teacher, so they were a little later than the other children. That wasn't a problem, since Nellie would have had to wait twenty minutes for the bus otherwise.

Robbie didn't know that school had been let out early, though, and he was not very happy. "What took you so long? We missed the bus," he said, his little voice trembling.

Nellie was sorry she had forgotten about her little brother; she should have thought of him. Her mother was always reminding her to keep an eye on him. She put her arm around him and said comfortingly, "No, we didn't miss the bus. School got out early today."

"Oh," said Robbie and pushed her arm away. He wasn't worried anymore now that his sister was there, and he didn't want to look like a baby.

"Just think. Two weeks of vacation!" he said, trying to sound important. "And I'm going to Grandma and Grandpa's," he told Lydia.

"Yes, but they're coming to our house first," Nellie added.

"Hey, Lydia," she said, "ask if you can come to our house the day after Christmas. We have an afternoon Christmas service for children at our church, something like we had today, except much nicer! There will be stories and singing and —"

"You'll get a book and candy!" Robbie interrupted, worried that Nellie might forget what he thought was the most important part.

"You'll ask, won't you?" Nellie begged, waiting for Lydia's answer.

"I would like to," Lydia said longingly. "But you know how my aunts are," she finished.

Nellie blushed. She was sorry she had brought it up. She should have known that Lydia wouldn't be allowed to go. She couldn't do anything! It was too bad Lydia had to live with those two strange aunts. Nellie felt sorry for her. She couldn't imagine what it must be like to live in such a house. She looked impatiently to see whether the bus was coming yet.

Robbie suddenly shouted, "Just sneak away! Don't even say anything to those two old —"

"Robbie!" Nellie warned him sternly.

"Well, they're two old witches. You think so yourself!"

Robbie looked triumphantly at his sister, who glared back at him.

"I'm going to tell Mother. You shouldn't be so —"

"Oooooh! Tattletale!"

"Okay, you guys, here comes the bus," Lydia said in relief. She was embarrassed by their bickering and comments about her aunts. Robbie had shouted so loudly that some of the other kids waiting for the bus had turned around and started laughing.

"I'm going. Bye!" she called, not waiting as she usually did for Nellie and Robbie to get on the bus. She walked slowly down the street and past the brightly lit shop windows.

Oh! That Robbie and his big mouth! It had been such a nice afternoon, and now he and Nellie had spoiled everything. Why had Nellie asked her to come to that program anyway? She knew very well that Lydia wasn't allowed to go to such things.

Lydia stopped to look in a bookstore window. There lay "her" Bible. Oh, how she wished she could have it. Every time she walked past this store, she looked at it.

Nellie had a children's Bible, but it didn't have colored pictures like this one. There were two of them in the store window. One Bible was closed, but the other one lay open, showing a picture of Joseph and Mary on their way to Bethlehem. It was such a beautiful picture!

Lydia wondered how much a Bible like that would cost. She considered stepping inside and asking, but what good would that do since she didn't have the money for it?

Nellie had gotten a children's Bible from her grandparents when she turned eight, but at Lydia's house birthdays were never observed. She didn't even know when her aunts' birthdays were. The kids at school thought it was weird that Lydia's family didn't celebrate birthdays.

Lydia still blushed when she remembered the time in second grade when her teacher had said, "It's your birthday today, isn't it, Lydia?" Lydia had been shocked because she hadn't even known it was her birthday! All day long the children had pestered her with comments like, “Hey! You didn’t pass out a birthday treat!” and “How come you didn’t know it was your birthday? How could you forget your own birthday?”

Lydia stopped to look in a bookstore window.

Lydia had been so embarrassed she had wanted to run away and hide. Why had the teacher mentioned her birthday and made the whole class laugh at her? For a few days Lydia had been very upset with her teacher, but as the kids forgot about it, Lydia forgave her teacher.

While she stood by the bookstore window, dreaming, she was pushed aside by some boys. “Move over! We want to see!”

Lydia walked away without bothering to respond. Her steps quickened as she left the busy shopping area. She was starting to get cold!

Then she heard a loud voice behind her. “Hey, Lydia!” She turned around and saw Casey, the neighbor’s grandson, running toward her. She stopped and waited for him to catch up.

“We came to pick up Grandma,” he said, walking along with Lydia, “but I went to the post office and got some new stamps. I bought five new ones. Do you want to see them?”

“Sure.”

They stopped, and Casey proudly showed her his new stamps. “I bet there aren’t very many people who have these stamps. They’re worth a lot!” He carefully put them back into the envelope.

“Did you still have school today?” he asked, changing the subject.

“Yes, but we hardly did anything all day. This afternoon we had a Christmas program. The teacher told the class a nice story, and some of the children played flutes, and —”

"Oh," Casey interrupted her, "tonight we're having a Christmas party at our club. That's much nicer than your school's program. I —"

"How do you know?" Lydia exclaimed indignantly. "You've never been there!"

Ignoring her interruption, Casey continued, "I have to play the accordion all by myself. My father says I'm really talented; otherwise, they wouldn't have picked me. There are going to be a lot of important people at the party, and I think the mayor is going to be there, too!"

"Bragger," Lydia thought. He was always bragging about something, and she didn't believe half of what he said.

As they turned onto their street, Casey suddenly said, "Hey, this afternoon someone came to visit your aunts — a man with a whopper of a car, a new Mercedes. It was so big that other cars could hardly get past it. Boy, what a beauty! Some day I'm going to have one just like it."

"What did you say? Someone came to *my* house?" Lydia asked, her eyes widening in surprise.

"Yes, I saw the car stop at your house."

"Do you remember anything else?"

"Well, it was dark red, with wide, chrome —"

"No, no! I mean about the man!"

"Oh, the man. Sorry, I didn't really pay attention to him. Well, here's my grandma's house. See you later!"

******

Lydia rang the doorbell, and as she waited for the familiar sound of her aunt's shuffling feet, she wondered who the man could be. No one ever came to their house. Her thoughts were interrupted by the door's opening and her aunt's usual grumbling, "Oh, it's you. You're late!"

When Lydia entered the living room, she immediately saw that Aunt Trudy's chair was empty. "Where's Aunt Trudy?" she asked in surprise.

"In bed. Headache," came the curt reply.

Lydia sat down at her place by the table. She thought about the man who had been there. Who could it have been? Wait! Maybe it was the doctor. He probably came for Aunt Trudy. She went into the kitchen and asked, "What did the doctor say, Auntie?"

Her aunt was standing on a chair, washing the window above the counter.

"What?" she asked, looking shocked.

"What did the doctor say?"

"Doctor…doctor? What doctor?" Aunt Kate snapped.

"Well, didn't the doctor come for Aunt Trudy?"

"Why, no!" Aunt Kate was now furiously wiping the window.

"Then who was the man who came here?" Lydia asked curiously.

There was complete silence for a minute.

"How do you…?" Aunt Kate began, but then she said, "No man has been here. Quit your whining and get out of the kitchen."

With a sigh, Lydia walked back to the table and sat down. She still didn't know anything. Maybe Casey had been wrong, and the man had gone to someone else's house while Casey was busy staring at the car. Boys were always interested in cars. That's all they talked about! They were always bragging about whose father had the biggest, best car.

Lydia decided to go upstairs and get her book. She was almost done with it. If she finished it tonight, she could bring it to Nellie's house tomorrow and ask for a new one. She came back downstairs with her book and had barely made herself comfortable when she heard Aunt Trudy's voice from the bedroom. "Kate? Kate?"

"Aunt Kate, Aunt Trudy is calling you."

"Oh, oh." Aunt Kate quickly climbed down from the chair and disappeared into the bedroom, closing the door behind her. Both of her aunts slept in that little bedroom. It was very drab and dark in there, since the drapes were usually closed, just as the door was now closed. Lydia couldn't hear what was being said behind that door and made no effort to listen. She knew it wasn't any of her business.

Everyone in this house went about her own business. There was never time for a decent conversation. Aunt Trudy slept most of the day with her knitting lying on her lap. Aunt Kate did nothing but work—morning, afternoon, evening—day in and day out.

And Lydia? She went to school. When she came home at four o'clock, she usually drew pictures or read a book. Once in a while she was allowed to play outside, and sometimes she had to do some shopping. At exactly seven-thirty, she went to bed. That was the way it had always been, and Lydia was used to it. But now that she was older and realized most kids didn't live like that, she wished things were different. She wished she could talk about anything she wanted to at home, that she could play outside when she wanted to, that she could bring a friend to her house, and that she could have some nice toys to play with. Sometimes she became angry and frustrated, while other times she felt hurt and very, very lonely. She often cried herself to sleep at night.

No one knew this, though. At school, she was known as cheerful Lydia, with her beautiful blond curls and her dark blue eyes. She was well liked by her classmates and was usually in the center of everything. Sometimes she even got into trouble and had to write lines secretly in her room in the attic, as a punishment from her teacher.

She didn't know that the teachers often commented to each other, "That Lydia surely can be mischievous, but she is really a sweet girl. It's too bad that she has such an antisocial home with those strange aunts. They keep her only because of the money they get. It's unbelievable how that girl can be so cheerful all the time. She brings sunshine into the classroom."

But they didn't know that once she came home from school, that "sunshine in the classroom" often felt very lonely and sad.

No one knew that.

Well, there was One—One who hears and sees everything. He knew of her troubles, and Lydia could tell Him of her sadness. The Lord can do all things, and He could help her, for He is a Father also of the fatherless.

CHAPTER 3

It was Monday morning, and Lydia was leaving the bakery after finally finishing all her shopping. She took a quick look at her list and mentally checked off the grocery store, the dairy, and the bakery. She hadn't forgotten anything.

She could tell it was the day before Christmas. Everyone was busy with last minute shopping, and there were long lines, especially at the bakery. She had to hurry, though, because Aunt Kate had told her to come right home after she was done. Her aunt was not herself today but was acting very strangely.

In fact, quite a few things had been strange the last few days. For one thing, Aunt Trudy was still in bed. Even though Lydia had bought some aspirin for her on Saturday, she didn't appear to be improving much.

Then there was Aunt Kate. She just wasn't herself — she seemed very mixed up and nervous. On Saturday, and again yesterday, Lydia had caught Aunt Kate just staring at her. When Lydia caught her eye, she quickly looked away. It was really odd. Her aunt had never behaved this way before.

On Saturday afternoon, the strangest thing had happened. Just as Lydia was hoping she could go outside to play, Aunt Kate had come inside with a newspaper. She had laid it on the table, pointed to an advertisement, and said, "Go buy this dress, a blue one. Make sure there's nothing wrong with it." Lydia couldn't believe her ears! Just like that she was told to go alone and buy a new dress!

Whenever Lydia needed new clothes, her aunt always went along. In fact, she got new clothes only when it was absolutely necessary, so she was not expecting something like this. Her clothes weren't in great shape, but she had thought they would have to last the rest of the winter. What a surprise! Feeling quite proud of herself, she had walked to the store and asked where she might find the dress that was shown in the advertisement. She was told that it was a special sale and only a couple of them were still left, one in green and another in blue.

Lydia had tried on the blue dress, and the saleslady said it looked very nice on her. When Lydia looked in the mirror, she thought so, too. She had never owned such a nice dress before, and it made her feel like a princess. When she got home, she tried on the dress again, and Aunt Kate seemed satisfied with it.

"When may I wear it?" Lydia had asked.

"When I tell you, that's when!" Aunt Kate had snapped.

Lydia had hoped she would be allowed to wear it on Sunday, but Aunt Kate had said nothing more about it.

******

On Saturday, Aunt Kate had washed Lydia's underwear and socks, and yesterday she had ironed and mended whatever needed mending. Her aunt had never been so busy doing things for her. Lydia wondered what all this attention meant.

Last night she had been sent to bed quite early, but she didn't fall asleep until it was very late. Then she was surprised to be awakened by Aunt Kate standing next to her bed this morning. "Get up, and put this on," she had said, pointing to the clean underwear and new dress. Lydia had looked at all those clean clothes in wonder. She couldn't understand why she was to wear a new dress on Monday, especially since it was a vacation day. It didn't make any sense.

While Lydia washed up in the kitchen, Aunt Kate stood right behind her, watching her every move. It was enough to make Lydia incredibly nervous!

Afterward, Aunt Kate said, "Just let your hair hang loose." Then, "Give me that comb!" and she yanked the comb out of Lydia's hand and began furiously combing her hair. Lydia was so stunned she was unable to say a word. She had never been allowed to wear her hair loose before.

When she was younger, Aunt Kate had always braided her hair, sometimes very, very tightly. But one day she had decided that Lydia was old enough to braid her own hair. Trying to braid her own hair had been a struggle for Lydia, because she could never do it neatly enough to please Aunt Kate. Finally her aunt told her just to comb her hair into two ponytails. "Don't you ever get it into your head to walk around with your hair hanging loose," she had threatened. And now this morning she was ordered to wear it loose. How very, very strange!

After much combing, Lydia's hair finally met with Aunt Kate's approval. She looked at Lydia from every angle and mumbled something that Lydia didn't understand. Lydia was just glad to be done with all the fussing, which made her uncomfortable and hot. She quickly sat down at the table to eat the sandwich that Aunt Kate had prepared for her.

After breakfast Lydia was sent to do some grocery shopping. Before she left, Aunt Kate made her put a coat on over her pretty new dress, and then sent her off with a final warning, "Now *please hurry*! You're already late."

Despite the fact that it was still quite early, there were a lot of shoppers already on the street and in the stores, and Lydia was detained everywhere she went. She was finally finished now and ready to head home.

As she left the bakery, Lydia noticed the sky was clear and the sun was shining brightly, but it was very cold! It was probably freezing. She remembered the two boys she had overheard at the bakery commenting, “Another night of frost like last night, and we can go skating.” She thought it sounded like fun to go skating, but she didn’t have any skates, and there was no way she could ever buy any.

Lydia walked slowly through the busy streets with her heavy shopping bags. Aunt Kate had told her to hurry, but she wasn’t overly worried about the warning since Aunt Kate always said that to her.

As she walked along, she thought about Aunt Kate’s strange behavior recently. She wondered about her new dress and why she had to wear it today. She also wondered why Aunt Kate had spent so much time with her hair. Why did she have to wear her hair loose instead of in ponytails? What was going on?

She passed a street organ and stopped to listen for a little while. She loved listening to the music, especially the Christmas music that was playing now. The notes of “Silent Night” filled the air and warmed her heart on this cold morning. Then she wondered if it was mockery. Normally the organ played worldly music, but now it was playing songs about the Lord Jesus. It didn’t seem as if those two really went together.

“Sounds nice, doesn’t it?” said the man with the street organ as he rattled his coin container. Lydia just smiled and continued walking.

******

The South Church clock struck once as she entered her street. She couldn't believe it was already ten-thirty. She had been gone a long time, and her aunt was going to be very irritated with her.

She hurried down the quiet street, but suddenly stopped. Could it be? Was that a big, dark red car standing in front of her house?

It certainly was! That had to be the same car that Casey was telling her about on Friday afternoon, and it was parked right in front of her door!

Aunt Kate had known somebody was coming. That's why she had been acting so strangely, and that's why Lydia had to be so neatly dressed today.

Who could it be? Someone from school?

No, no one from school had such a fine car. The doctor? According to Aunt Kate, he hadn't been there on Friday.

As she walked by the car, she looked at it curiously, as if the car could answer her questions. Then it suddenly occurred to her: the public school! How could she have forgotten!

Of course, that was it. Her aunts had threatened to send her to the public school, but since they hadn't said any more about it, she hoped they had forgotten or changed their minds. She was obviously mistaken. Aunt Kate must have called them from the telephone booth a couple of streets over, and now the principal was coming to talk to them. That's what was happening! Lydia was tempted to stay outside and keep walking. If she didn't come back until twelve o'clock, maybe the strange man would be gone. Or would he wait until she came home?

Just as she was trying to decide what to do, whether to ring the doorbell or leave, the door opened, and Aunt Kate, her cheeks flushed, said nervously, "Where have you been? I've looked out the window a hundred times to see if you were coming! Hurry up and come inside. Leave your shoes on."

With her heart pounding, Lydia went inside. How strange, how unusual, how mysterious! She sensed something important was about to happen.

Lydia could hear a man's voice and then her aunt's sharp voice answering, "Yes, of course, sir." Then she stepped into the room. There, in Aunt Trudy's chair beside the stove, sat a heavy-set man with black, shiny hair and big, gold-colored glasses.

He looked at Lydia, who remained standing hesitantly by the door. "Well, well," he called out in a rough voice, "a duplicate of Esther. Two peas in a pod. Child, child, it's as if I see your mother in front of me. Come here a minute."

"Yes," Lydia's aunt urged her, "shake hands. Come on, hurry up!"

Reluctantly Lydia went to the man, and as she looked at him, she wondered who this man could be who seemed to know her mother so well. He couldn't be from the public school. Besides, he had such a strange accent. She could understand it, but still....

He grabbed her hand firmly. "So you are Lydia Van Arkel. I came Friday, and the bird had flown the coop! I came today, and the bird almost escaped again! But now I have you. I'm sure your aunt has already told you who I am."

Lydia shook her head, and her aunt quickly explained, "No, I kept it a surprise."

"A surprise? Well, young lady, then I will tell you. But, let's go sit at the table so I can show you something. And, Auntie, the coffee was delicious. Please pour me another cup for good measure. Ha, ha, ha." His laugh resounded harshly through the tiny room. It sounded strange; laughter was never heard in this house.

Lydia was still puzzled. She didn't understand what was happening, but that man acted as if he were right at home here. He just asked for coffee, and her aunt jumped to get it for him.

When they were all seated around the table, he began to explain. "Lydia, I am Mr. Russell from the circus where your father and mother performed. It's too bad that you never really knew them, child, but they were real artists! They were known and loved by everyone, so it was a heavy blow to lose them. They were such an important part of the circus.

"Your aunt has told me you don't have any pictures of them, so that means you don't know about your parents' beautiful work. But I will show you something."

He picked up the briefcase standing beside his chair, pulled out a pile of magazines and pictures, and then drew his chair closer to Lydia's. "Look," he said, opening a magazine. "Here is a picture of your father and mother!"

Lydia stared at the big, colored picture. Were those people walking on a tightrope, high up in the air, her parents? Oh, how scary and dangerous! Lydia was stunned.

More pictures followed, but Lydia didn't like them at all. She had never pictured Papa and Mama like that. They had such strange clothes! Some pictures made them look as if they were floating through the air. Lydia was shocked.

Meanwhile, Mr. Russell kept talking. “Look, Lydia, this is a French magazine. The headline says: ‘Esther and John Dance Through Life.’ That’s how it was. They were artists—first-class tightrope walkers, and it was the joy of their lives!”

When they had finished looking at all the pictures, Mr. Russell stirred his coffee and asked, “What do you think of them?”

It was quiet for a moment. Aunt Kate had joined them at the table, and her piercing eyes looked at Lydia. She was about to speak when Lydia answered with a soft, trembling voice, “I don’t like them!”

“What?” the man exclaimed in surprise. “You don’t like them? I don’t understand at all. Any child would be proud of such parents!”

Aunt Kate stammered, “Of course, y-you have to like it. Tell him that-that…you think they’re nice!”

Lydia blinked back a few tears and tried hard not to cry.

Those strange people were her father and mother? Papa’s letter had given her a whole different impression. She had imagined them to be much like Nellie’s father and mother, but these pictures showed people who didn’t look at all like Nellie’s parents. She couldn’t imagine Nellie’s mother looking so strange. She wished she had never seen the pictures. What was Mr. Russell doing here, anyway?

Mr. Russell threw his arm around Lydia’s shoulder and said to her muttering aunt, “Quiet, Auntie, quiet. I said that I couldn’t understand it, but I really can understand it a little. And, Lydia, I actually have to be a bit upset with your aunt. Auntie, don’t look at me so surprised. The pictures are all new and strange for this young lady. She's not used to circuses. You should have talked with her about them and taken her with you when the circus came to town! Don't worry; she'll get used to this.

"Lydia, listen. If your father and mother were still living, you would have had a whole different life and grown up in the circus family. The children of our artists travel along with their parents. We have our own little school, and most of the children have inherited their parents' talents. If they are interested in the work, we train them well. That is what would have happened with you, too, if it hadn't been for that unfortunate accident. You were taken in by relatives, and we lost contact with you. Our old manager couldn't forget you, though, and he thought a child of Esther and John must have some of their talent. He has often asked me to look for you, but life in a circus is a busy one of traveling and packing, so nothing has come of it until now.

"Right now our circus is in France, but since I had to go to Belgium and the Netherlands unexpectedly, the manager asked me to find you and bring you back with me. I've been searching, and here I am. I came just in time, because your aunts are getting older, and they won't be able to take care of you much longer.

"Not only that, it's better for you to be in a young family. We have several children about your age. Wouldn't you like to have friends your own age to play with all the time? Besides, you will learn how to dance and could become as famous as your father and mother! Well, Lydia, what do you think of that?"

After listening to the whole story, Lydia didn't know what to think. Was she dreaming? Was that man really there in the house? Did she have to go with him to the circus? She swallowed hard. Her throat was dry, and the man was very close to her. Suddenly she stood up and hoarsely cried out, "I won't do it! I won't go along!"

Aunt Kate stood up, too, and started to interrupt again, but Mr. Russell hushed her and said, "Quiet! Lydia, you don't know what you are refusing. Your father and mother would have loved to know that you're following in their footsteps. When you were born, your father said proudly, 'A little dancer!' I know that you would certainly disappoint them if you don't go along. As I said earlier, it was the joy of their life to dance, and it should be the same for you. This evening I'm going back to France, and you may go with me. Everyone in the circus will accept you with open arms. Child, you look so much like your mother!"

Lydia didn't let him continue. She didn't like the man and wasn't going to listen to him any longer. She certainly would *not* go with him.

"No!" she exclaimed, hardly able to keep from bursting into tears. "I will not join the circus. Papa himself wrote in his letter to me that I should never do it, because…."

"Keep still," Aunt Kate screamed, but Lydia didn't listen and, with fits and starts, continued, "The circus…is…mockery, and…and the Lord doesn't…approve of…of it either."

Mr. Russell looked at her in astonishment. His thoughts raced through his mind. She had a letter from her father, and he had written that she should never go to the circus? It was true Esther and John were completely changed while they lay in the hospital. They had suddenly wanted nothing more to do with the circus. He remembered that well, but he hadn't thought too much about it recently. The circus people had heard this news from the minister who had cared for Esther and John. It seemed the two tightrope walkers were very sick and had believed everything the minister had said. And now Lydia believed it, too.

Mr. Russell stood up and laid his hand on Lydia's shoulder. "Listen, child, your father did not know what he was writing when he was sick. We don't mock. And if there is a God, as you say, then you have His permission to dance. You are young and shouldn't be so worried about that."

"Sir, take her along with you now. She doesn't have any choice in the matter. Such a…" Aunt Kate's voice shrilled nervously.

But Lydia angrily pushed Mr. Russell's hand away. "It *is* mocking, and I will *never* do it. I will *never* dance. And…and I will run away. I…I…" and then she began to cry.

As Lydia tried to flee from the room, her aunt grabbed her by the arm. "Stay here! You are going! Do you hear? You're going along!"

Mr. Russell watched silently. He could see there was no persuading Lydia. He had expected her to dance around the room with joy when she heard she could go along with him. Who wouldn't want to trade such a dreary life with two peculiar aunts for the exciting life of a circus! Such a stubborn child! He hadn't expected that at all.

He was becoming impatient with Lydia now and worried about what might happen if he brought her to the circus and she refused to learn. It was also possible that she wouldn't be talented enough to perform for them, and then they would be stuck with her. He watched Lydia sobbing as she tried to break loose from her aunt's firm grip and heard her cry, "I'm not going along. I won't do it!" He made up his mind, collected the magazines and pictures from the table, and stuffed them in his briefcase, saying, "I've said enough and have to leave now. Let her stay. I'll come back in a couple of years to talk about it some more. Goodbye!" He hastily left the room.

Aunt Kate called to him, "But, sir! Sir, she's going along. She has no choice. Come on, Lydia, tell him you'll go. Right now. Hurry up!"

Instead, they heard the front door close. Mr. Russell was gone.

There was complete silence for a moment. Then the bedroom door opened, Aunt Trudy's head appeared around the corner, and she whined, "Won't she go?"

Aunt Kate was so furious that she could hardly speak. Her face was bright red, and she glared at Lydia with eyes full of hatred. Then she screamed, "Get out of here! Out!"

Lydia barely managed to grab her jacket off the hook as she was shoved out the door, stumbling and nearly falling over the step. The front door slammed behind her, and she ran blindly down the street. She ran and ran until she was so tired she had to slow down.

Lydia's face felt tight from her tears and from the cold air. As she looked at her surroundings, she realized she was close to a park quite a distance from her home. She didn't know why she had run so far. After all, Aunt Kate couldn't have chased after her. Since she had nowhere else to go, she went into the park.

It was very quiet in the park. It was too cold for most people to be out walking, but Lydia didn't feel the cold. She saw a little concrete bench and sat down. It had been a terrible morning, and she was exhausted.

Lydia was sorry the man had come to her house, and she imagined what would have happened if he had grabbed her and said, “You have to go along whether you like it or not.” It would have been awful to have been forced to go to France and live among strangers.

That man had showed her very unpleasant pictures. One was of a man standing between two lions. It gave her shivers just thinking about it, but the pictures of Papa and Mama were the worst. The thought of those made her want to cry. She would not like a father and mother like that. When she returned home, she would read Papa’s letter, because that was the father she loved. She was sure he had written in the letter that she should never go to a circus.

When she went home, then—oh, no, what home? When would she be able to go home? She had been sent away! Now Lydia was afraid. What if she weren’t allowed in the house anymore? Where would she go? She had nowhere else to go! There she sat under a big chestnut tree, all alone in the park, feeling lonely and very cold.

Lydia folded her cold hands, bowed her head, and prayed, “Lord, please help me. I don’t know where I must go. Aunt Kate is angry, but I won’t go to the circus. I will never do it, because it is not good. Help me, Lord, for Jesus’ sake. Amen.”

Lydia folded her cold hands.

CHAPTER 4

Lydia was almost to Nellie's house. The familiar walk seemed to be much farther than usual because of the cold. Besides, she was starting to feel sick, either because she hadn't eaten for a while or because she felt so abandoned.

Lydia had finally left the park because she was so cold. She had walked to the main street and found a department store. She wandered around inside for a while, stopping on every floor, but nothing interested her. Normally, she would have loved looking at everything, especially the toys, but this time her thoughts kept returning to what had happened that morning: to Mr. Russell, to the circus, and to Aunt Kate, who had sent her away.

As she was leaving the department store, Lydia had noticed a man making waffles near the entrance. She had watched him a while, enjoying the warmth and the wonderful smell of the fresh waffles. She was amazed at how quickly and efficiently he could make the delicious treats.

When he saw her watching him, he had curtly asked, "Do you want one?" Lydia had shaken her head. "Well, move along then. You're standing in the way of my customers," he had snapped, "and don't plan on getting any free handouts."

Lydia had walked away, her facing burning with humiliation. It seemed as if everybody was sending her away or treating her unkindly. She was feeling even lonelier than before.

At that point she had decided to go to Nellie's house. She always felt welcome there, and maybe Nellie's mother would be able to help her solve her problems. In fact, Nellie's parents might even ask Lydia to stay with them. That would be perfect.

Nellie lived in a new neighborhood that was still being developed; her house was one of the few that were finished. There were many homes still in the process of being built, but the work had been put on hold because of the weather.

Lydia's intentions were to go straight to Nellie's house, but instead she saw Nellie and Robbie playing with a group of children. The kids were making a long ice slide on some frozen puddles in the middle of the field. Lydia ran over to them.

"Hey, Lydia! It's great you came!" Nellie said in surprise

"We're making a slide. Want to help?" Robbie called out to her. His cheeks were rosy from the cold.

Lydia didn't really feel like playing and would have preferred to go straight to Nellie's house. She longed for a warm, cozy house, and she really wanted to discuss her problems with Nellie's mother. Then she decided to be patient and join the others. She would play with them and act as though nothing were wrong

They all took turns sliding down the icy strip; all except Robbie, that is. The other kids thought he was too little to play with them, so they always left him out.

Finally a girl with long, dark hair called out, "I've had enough. Nellie, let's go."

Nellie turned to go with her. Lydia recognized the girl as Carla, who was staying with her aunt and uncle, Nellie's neighbors. Nellie had talked about her before.

When Carla stayed by her aunt, she spent a lot of time at Nellie's house.

Lydia was disappointed that Carla was there. She would much rather spend time alone with Nellie. With Carla around, Lydia couldn't tell them about her aunt sending her away. She hoped Carla would go home soon!

By now the other children had stopped sliding. They all seemed to have become tired of it. "Let's play hide-and-seek," one of the boys called out. Most of the others agreed.

Quickly one of them was chosen to stand behind a tree and count while the others found places to hide. Nick was *It.* He began counting: "One, two, three…."

The children ran in all directions. Carla pulled Nellie along with her. Robbie, the youngest, followed, but Carla said, "Go somewhere else. We don't want you with us."

Lydia noticed and called, "Come here, Robbie!" She took him by the hand, and together they crouched behind a fence.

"It's not fair that Carla sent me away, is it, Lydia?" Robbie whispered.

"No," Lydia agreed. "Just stay with me, okay? I know some good hiding places."

The game lasted a long time. There were several good hiding places, and sometimes it took fifteen minutes to find everyone. The children were having a good time and kept playing even as the sun began to set and the air started getting colder.

When it was Lydia's turn to be *It*, Robbie wanted to help her.

"No," Nellie told him, "you have to go hide, too," and she ran after Carla. Robbie started to follow them but changed his mind. He ran off alone, letting the girls go by themselves.

"Ready or not, here I come!" Lydia hollered. She didn't hear anyone, so she started looking around. She wondered where Robbie was, and decided that she would act as if she didn't see him if she did find him. She'd let him beat her to the tree. He was always left out because he was the youngest. Nobody ever let him win.

Then she saw someone crouching down behind a car. It was a girl in a red jacket. Lydia thought her name was Hannah or Janna, or something like that.

"Free!" she heard from behind the tree. It came from Nellie and Carla. Then Gerrit and René came running out from behind a construction office. Lydia raced over, but the boys were just ahead of her.

After they all reached the tree and stood there debating who had been first, Carla exclaimed, "Hey, Robbie's not here yet!"

It was true. Lydia went looking for him again, but Robbie was nowhere to be found.

"Let's just keep playing," René suggested.

"No way. Robbie's part of the game, too," Lydia protested.

Finally, a couple of girls decided it was time to go home.

"I don't really feel like playing anymore, either," René said and ambled off with his hands in his pockets. His friend Gerrit followed closely behind.

"If everyone is leaving, I'm not going to play. Without those two it's no fun," Carla said. The others agreed.

"R-o-b-b-i-e!! Come out! We're done," they called. But Robbie didn't appear.

"You go look behind the construction office, and I'll look behind that fence," Lydia offered.

After about five minutes of searching, they met back at the tree. "Let's quit looking. He must have heard us by now," Carla said, but Nellie was a little worried. She didn't want to leave Robbie out there alone.

"Let's look again. He was hiding with you before, wasn't he, Lydia? What places did you hide?"

"Behind that fence and there in the firebreak. We were never far from the tree," Lydia answered.

"Would he have gone to the construction site? Maybe we should try there," Nellie said and ran off, with Carla and Lydia behind her. A short, nervous guard was walking around the site. He saw the girls coming and asked them what they were doing there.

"Sir," Nellie called, "have you seen a little boy wearing a brown jacket and green cap wandering around here?"

"All I've seen are a bunch of troublesome kids. Get out of here," he snarled.

"Yes, but sir…sir, we can't find him," Lydia protested.

"Well, you can't look here."

There they stood.

"Okay, let's stop looking," Carla decided. "It's his own fault if he hid so far away."

"No, it's your fault. You should have taken him along with you," Lydia said.

Nellie didn't know what to say, but she didn't dare to go home until she found Robbie. Even though he could be a nuisance at times, she knew she would be in big trouble if he weren't found soon. "R-o-b-b-i-e!" she called again. There was no answer to her call. By this time, all the other children had gone home, and it was very quiet.

"You can keep looking, but I'm going home," Carla said with resolve. "I'm sure he'll show up if we stop looking for him. He's probably just trying to make us mad."

Nellie hesitated. She really wanted to go home. It was very cold, and it was getting dark. "Okay, let's go," she said. "Do you want to come over? We can play the new game I got from my grandma and grandpa."

Lydia hoped Carla would say "No," but she didn't. Instead she followed Nellie down the street.

"What time do you have to be home, Lydia?" Nellie asked.

"Oh…um…um…it doesn't matter."

All of a sudden, Lydia started to feel afraid and very lonely. All afternoon she had tried to forget about the terrible scare she had experienced that morning. She had comforted herself with the thought that soon she would be able to tell Nellie's mother everything. Nellie's mother would know what to do. But now Carla was going to be there, too. Who knew how long she would stay? Lydia wasn't going to say anything while Carla was there. It was none of her business.

******

Lydia walked silently along with Nellie and Carla, who chattered happily together as they walked. Lydia didn't hear much of what they were saying, because she was deep in her own thoughts.

As they came to the gate leading to Nellie's yard, Lydia stopped. She didn't know if she should go in with them. Besides, she wasn't at all in the mood to play a game.

"Come on!" Nellie invited as she held the gate open, so Lydia went along in spite of her misgivings. She thought a warm house might make her feel better. She was chilled to the bone.

Nellie's mother was pouring coffee in the kitchen. "What do we have here? Three cold faces! Hi, Lydia! How did you dare come way over here in the cold? I'll make a mug of hot chocolate for each of you right away," she said warmly.

"Do we have visitors?" Nellie asked, looking at all the mugs her mother had laid out.

"Yes, Uncle Frank and Aunt Wilma have come to see Grandpa and Grandma. Carla's aunt was here earlier, too. We were just talking about the fact that you were staying out so long in the cold. Robbie's been home for a while already. It was getting too cold for him."

"See. Did you hear that?" Carla said and gave Nellie a poke as they took off their jackets in the hallway.

"What?"

"Your mother said that Robbie has been home for a while already!"

"He's home?" Nellie asked in surprise, and they burst out laughing. "How dumb! None of us even thought that Robbie might have gone home."

"And we were searching all over in the cold!" Nellie sighed. "How dumb of us!"

"And I thought you were always so bright," Carla said, laughing. "You disappoint me!"

It was warm and cozy in the living room, and everyone was busy talking. Nellie's father was there, and sitting at the table, Robbie was playing with Legos. The girls watched him for a few minutes.

"I'm making our neighborhood," he said. "Look, these are the houses that are still being built, and this is the office."

"I hope you realize that we have to use the table, too. You can't take up the whole thing," Nellie said bossily.

"No way! All of this has to stay here. Mom, can I keep my stuff here?"

His mother, who was passing around mugs of coffee and talking with her company, didn't hear him.

"Oh, well," Carla said to Nellie, "let's go sit in your bedroom. It's quieter in there!"

Nellie went to her mother and asked, "Mom, may we play in my room? Robbie needs the whole table."

"Sure, go ahead, as long as you keep quiet. I just put Elise to bed upstairs for her nap. Here, take your hot chocolate with you. If you wait a minute, I'll give you a snack to go along with it."

******

A little while later they were seated in Nellie's cozy room. Nellie and Lydia sat on wicker chairs, while Carla sat on the bed. On the little table were their three mugs of steaming hot chocolate. The girls were quiet as they ate their cake. It tasted wonderful after playing in the cold air so long, especially to Lydia who had eaten nothing since morning.

When they finished, Nellie put the empty mugs and plates on the serving tray. As she left the room, she said, "I'll bring the tray downstairs and go get the game."

That left Carla and Lydia alone. Carla glanced at Lydia and then took a book from the bookcase and began paging through it. She acted as if Lydia weren't even there, and Lydia didn't try talking to her, either. As Lydia watched Carla sitting on the bed, she thought how strange the situation was. This was the first time she had met Carla, and already she didn't like her. The only reason was that Carla had ruined her plans. All afternoon Lydia had hoped Carla would go home and worried about what would happen if Carla didn't go. If Carla didn't leave, Lydia would have to leave Nellie's house without talking to Nellie's mother. She didn't want to play a game, and she wondered if she should just leave now. Then she heard quick footsteps coming up the stairs. Nellie was coming back with the game in her hand.

As Nellie entered the room, she flipped on the light and then turned up the heat, since it was starting to get chilly in her room. "Okay, let me read the rules," she said, setting the game down and pulling her chair closer to the little table.

"Oh, *that* game?" Carla asked. "I have that one at home. I've played it with my brothers so much I'm sick of it!"

"Come on. You can play it again with us," Nellie replied, a little offended. "Maybe these questions are different from the ones in your game. You want to play, don't you, Lydia?"

"Oh…um…yeah. How do you play?"

Nellie explained the rules. With a pained look, Carla took her turn. Reluctantly Lydia did, too, but her mind was not on the game. She couldn't answer even the easiest questions.

A tree that started with the letter "E"? Lydia had no idea.

"How dumb," Carla mocked. "Even Robbie would know that," she said, exaggerating. "Who hasn't heard of an elm tree!"

"Hey, cut it out!" Nellie exclaimed. "You just gave the answer!" Nellie was annoyed. Carla was making it very obvious that she wasn't enjoying the game, and Lydia wasn't acting normal, either. She was so quiet. Was she upset that Carla was there? Carla was usually pretty friendly. Okay, sometimes she was a little bossy, but most of the time they got along all right.

Before they even got halfway through the questions, Nellie gave up. "Let's quit. It's obvious you guys aren't interested in playing. Thanks a lot!"

"We could do something else," Carla suggested. Looking disappointed, Nellie returned the cards to the box.

Carla could tell that Nellie was irritated, so she quickly changed the subject. "Hey, Nellie, my uncle's going to talk at the Christmas program and read an interesting story. I have to say a text, but I haven't learned it yet. Have you learned yours? Maybe we could study them together tonight." Nellie's bad mood started wearing off as she and Carla talked excitedly about the upcoming Christmas program.

"Are you coming, too?" Carla suddenly asked Lydia, who had been quietly listening.

Lydia was startled. "Uh…I don't think so."

"Oh, I suppose you can't go," Carla said and gave Lydia a cold, mocking look. "I could never live with those two crabby old ladies!"

Lydia blushed. How did Carla know? She looked at Nellie, whose face was turning red. Nellie tried to change the subject, but Carla continued, "I would never be allowed to play with a circus child! Nellie's mother thinks it's terrible, too. She —"

"That's not true," Nellie objected. "My mother doesn't think it's bad at all!"

"What? I was right there when she said to my aunt, 'I would rather not have Nellie be friends with someone like that. She doesn't go to church and —'"

"Quit lying," Nellie exclaimed, her face turning red.

"Yeah, and you even said to me that you wouldn't dare play at her house because you thought her aunts were creepy!"

Lydia jumped up from her chair. She was hurt and terribly disappointed with Nellie. With a trembling voice, she said, "How unfair! How mean! How dare you talk about me when I'm not around! First to Robbie and now to her," and she nodded toward Carla. "Well, go ahead and play together. I won't be coming here any more. I think you're mean. I —"

Lydia couldn't continue, or she knew she'd start crying. She didn't want that to happen and have them laugh at her. Without another word, she ran out the room and down the stairs.

Fortunately, no one was around when she went downstairs, although she could hear laughing and talking in the living room. She put on her jacket and mittens, quietly opened and then closed the front door, and ran down the street. She didn't look back. She could just imagine Carla looking out the window, laughing at her. What a nasty girl!

Lydia was also shocked and hurt by Nellie, her best friend. She had always trusted Nellie and confided in her. She would never have guessed that Nellie would talk about her behind her back. Besides that, Nellie had laughed and mocked Lydia and told people that her aunts were strange and creepy. Lydia knew she would never go to Nellie's house again. Never! Nellie was two-faced and mean!

******

It was six-thirty when Lydia entered her street, tired and cold. She had wandered the streets for a long time. She was terribly afraid to go home, and yet she had to. What else could she do?

When she came to her street, she thought, I'll just walk around the block one more time, and then I'll go home. But after going around the block once, she still didn't dare, so she walked around again. She finally had to risk it, since she couldn't stay out on the street all night. She was worried about what would happen if Aunt Kate wouldn't let her in, but then decided she had to stop being such a worrywart. Maybe it wouldn't be as bad as she thought. Maybe her aunt's temper had cooled off.

Lydia tried to gather up her courage, but her heart pounded as she stood at the door. She started to reach for the doorbell, and then quickly pulled back her hand. Finally, she rang it. Ringggg! The noise startled her. It sounded much louder than usual.

While Lydia waited, she worried that it was taking longer than usual for the door to open. She was sure her aunt could have opened it by now. What would she do if no one opened the door? Did she dare ring again? She started to reach for the bell a second time. Then she heard a shuffling noise, and the door opened a crack. She saw Aunt Kate's face for a second, but then it disappeared.

Lydia pushed the door open farther and entered the dark hallway to find that her aunt was already in the other room. She took off her jacket and shoes, happy to be inside at last.

Now what should she do? Lydia wondered whether she should go into the room or just go straight upstairs. Then she remembered she hadn't eaten yet and hoped her aunt had a plate ready for her. She walked into the living room, only to have her aunt snap at her, "Get to bed! How dare you come back here?" Then she called Lydia a nasty name.

Lydia ran from the living room and fled upstairs. Her bedroom in the attic was icy cold, and the light on the ceiling was dim. Shivering from the cold, Lydia undressed and tossed her pretty new dress over a chair. The joy of receiving a new dress had soured long ago. It didn't mean anything to her now.

Lydia bowed her knees by her bed and prayed, but her mind wandered. She was sad and lonely. Finally she turned off the light and crawled into bed, sliding deep under the blankets. Brrr. Everything was so cold. She buried her face in her pillow, trying not to think about the miserable day behind her. Not about Mr. Russell, who had wanted to take her with him to the circus, not about her angry aunt, and certainly not about the pictures of Papa and Mama.

As Lydia lay there, she remembered she was going to read Papa's letter. But she didn't feel like doing that, either. Lydia knew he had written that she should never go to a circus. She didn't want to think about the letter. Nor about Nellie.

When Christmas vacation was over and she had to go to school again, Lydia decided, she would act as if she didn't see Nellie. She wasn't going to have anything to do with her. That's for sure!

Tomorrow was Christmas. Lydia wondered how it would go. She was sure it wasn't going to be a good day for her. Nellie and Carla would be going to church together. She wished she could go. It would be nice to hear about the Lord Jesus, who was born in a manger in Bethlehem. He was so rich, but He had left everything for people who had been disobedient. A tear dropped onto Lydia's pillow.

In church they would sing:[1]

This is the light prepared to shine
Upon the Gentile lands;
Thine Israel's glory and their hope,
To break their slavish bands.

They sang that at school, too. She loved how it sounded. Another tear dropped onto her pillow, and another, and another. Lydia cried.

The wind shook the house, and the attic window rattled. The lonely girl in the bed paid no attention. She was feeling terribly sad. Who was able to help her?

The moon slipped behind some dark clouds. It couldn't shine through those thick clouds, but the Lord, who lives high in the heavens, could see through them. He can see and hear everything. He is a Father of the fatherless.

---

[1] *The Psalter*, Spiritual Songs, The Song of Simeon, Verse 4.

CHAPTER 5

"Hey, you lazy girl! Get down here!"

Lydia blinked. "No," she groaned, sleepily. "I don't want to."

"Get out of bed!"

Now Lydia was wide awake. She looked around in surprise. She had thought she was still at Nellie's house. The three of them had been sitting there together: Nellie, Carla, and Lydia. Then Carla had said, "You have to go along to the circus, don't you?"

"No way," Lydia had retorted.

"Yes, you do! Mr. Russell said so," Carla insisted.

She and Carla had begun arguing, while Nellie just sat there laughing and laughing. Then Aunt Kate's face had suddenly appeared around the corner. "Come on! You wanted to run away, didn't you? Hurry up. Come with me!"

Lydia had wanted to run away, but she couldn't go anywhere. She was so scared! Mr. Russell had come, too, along with Nellie's father and mother, and Lydia's teacher. They were all laughing and laughing at her. Lydia had looked for a way to escape, but she couldn't get away because it was slippery and everything was coated with ice. It was really strange. Her feet had kept slipping, and she had started to panic. All this time Aunt Kate was calling, "Come on! Aren't you coming?" Finally she had decided to climb out the bedroom window. She had to get away from all those laughing people. She had jumped and almost reached the ground when she awoke. What a relief! It was only a dream, but Lydia was all hot and sweaty.

"Don't you hear me?" came the call from downstairs. Aunt Kate! It really was Aunt Kate calling her.

"I'm coming!" Lydia threw off the blankets and jumped out of bed. The floor was freezing cold, and the little window in her room was covered with frost. Lydia could see that it was already light outside. She had slept a long time! She quickly dressed, happy to be allowed to go downstairs again.

Yesterday had been Christmas day, and Lydia had been forced to stay in the attic all day. In the morning, when she had started to go downstairs, Aunt Kate had stood below and snapped, "Get back up there, and don't let me see you all day." What a long, miserable day she had endured in the cold attic. She had pulled her blankets around her and sat on the bed most of the day. Once, Aunt Kate had called up to her, "Here, eat." On the bottom step Aunt Kate had placed a plate with three slices of slightly buttered bread and a glass half filled with milk. It was not much to eat for a whole day, but Lydia hadn't been very hungry anyway. Her stomach hadn't felt right, and she was very miserable and lonely.

Not knowing what else to do, Lydia had read Nellie's book again. She had also attempted drawing a picture, but that was too hard while sitting in bed. She had tried to think up different things to do, but nothing had lasted very long, and she had soon lost interest. The day had passed very slowly.

Last night it had been late before she finally fell asleep. She had drifted in and out, but kept waking up. She wondered how late it had been before she had finally fallen into a deep sleep. She was pretty sure it had been very late, and that was why she had slept so late this morning. Now, she was glad to be awake after such a terrifying dream.

******

Now it was the day after Christmas, and Auntie was calling her. Lydia was relieved that she was going to be allowed downstairs. She couldn't bear the thought of having to spend another day in that cold attic.

Lydia was nervous as she went down the steps with the plate and glass in her hand. She didn't know what she should say to her aunt when she saw her. She hoped Auntie would be in a better mood this morning. Aunt Kate's anger must have cooled, or else she wouldn't have called her downstairs.

Lydia peeked into the living room, but Aunt Kate was nowhere to be seen. Aunt Trudy's chair was empty, too, making Lydia wonder if she was still sick. Maybe that was where Aunt Kate was, since Lydia didn't see her in the kitchen either.

Lydia washed up and combed her pretty blond curls. She had trouble getting the comb through them because they were all tangled from the last couple of days. She wondered if she should just let her hair hang loose again, but decided she had better braid it. On Monday, she had been told to let her hair hang loose, but that was for Mr. Russell. Mr. Russell would not be here today. He'd be back in France by now, and he could stay there!

Finally, she was finished. Her hair wasn't as neat as usual, but that didn't really matter. She went back into the living room. There on the table she found a plate with two pieces of bread and a cup of tea. The cup was hers, so the food must be for her, too. She looked at the clock. It was already quarter to ten!

When Lydia finished eating, she cleared the table. She was seated in her usual chair, gazing out the window, when Aunt Kate came from the little bedroom. Lydia didn't know what to do or say, so she just remained silent. Aunt Kate didn't say anything, either, but walked straight to the kitchen, where she rummaged around for a while. Then, she came back through the living room and went up the stairs. Lydia didn't know what Aunt Kate was doing, but assumed that Aunt Kate was probably going to clean the attic and make Lydia's bed.

Lydia started to wonder what she would do if Aunt Kate didn't speak to her all day. Should she just stay sitting in her chair? There wasn't much else she could do.

Then Lydia suddenly remembered Aunt Trudy. Maybe she could go into Aunt Trudy's bedroom and find out how she was doing. Although Aunt Trudy was strange—even stranger than Aunt Kate—she hardly ever screamed. Aunt Kate was the one who made all the decisions, while Aunt Trudy just nodded her head in agreement!

Lydia stood up, and then changed her mind. If Aunt Trudy was sleeping or had a bad headache, it might not be a good idea after all. If Aunt Kate found out that Lydia had been in there, she would really get in trouble! With a sigh, she plunked herself back down onto her chair.

Lydia could hear Aunt Kate rummaging around upstairs. She was making a lot more noise than usual. There was bumping and banging going on that Lydia had never heard before! Then there was a dull thud that sounded as though Aunt Kate had fallen, followed by silence. After a little pause, Lydia heard more shuffling and banging. It almost sounded as if Aunt Kate were doing spring cleaning!

Lydia was starting to become very curious. She really wanted to take a peek at what was going on upstairs, but she didn't dare. She hoped her aunt wasn't digging through her drawers. She might find Papa's letter and tear it up. Lydia knew Aunt Kate wouldn't hesitate to do that! Lydia also worried about what Aunt Kate might do if she found Nellie's book or the Psalter and Bible she used for her schoolwork.

Lydia did not trust her aunt making all that noise upstairs. She thought about telling her that Aunt Trudy was calling. If Aunt Kate came down, Lydia could quickly run upstairs to see what she had been doing.

Then it was quiet for a minute, and Lydia listened tensely. After a moment, she heard footsteps and the squeaking of the stairs. Aunt Kate was coming down.

Lydia looked out the living room doorway in suspense. There was Aunt Kate with a yellow envelope in her hand. Papa's letter? No, his letter was in a white envelope. Her aunt disappeared with the envelope into Aunt Trudy's bedroom.

There was silence in the living room except for the ticking of the mantel clock. Lydia tried to think what might be in that envelope. A letter? She doubted that was it, because her aunts hardly ever received letters.

While Lydia was trying to guess what the envelope contained, the bedroom door opened again. It was Aunt Kate with the mysterious envelope still in her hand. She coughed, walked over to the cabinet where the dishes were kept, and then came to the table. She stood in front of Lydia, who had been watching her curiously and wondering what was going to happen next. It was obvious that something important was about to occur. Aunt Kate coughed again. Her eyes were blinking nervously, and the hand holding the envelope was shaking.

"Listen," she said in her shrill voice. "You are an arrogant child! You wouldn't go along with Mr. Russell, you were disrespectful, and I was ashamed of you! Is that how I brought you up? Did I teach you to be so rude? I've had enough. Do you hear me? I'm not going to put up with it any longer!"

She moved closer to Lydia, talking louder and louder, until they were face to face. Lydia jumped up in fear. Her aunt looked so threatening that Lydia was scared. She stepped backward, but her aunt kept moving closer.

"So you want to run away? Well, go ahead, you can leave now! I'm not putting up with you anymore. You're not going to get another penny from us. Do you understand? Here," and she whipped a card out of the envelope and stuck it under Lydia's nose. "You can go there. That's where you belong, anyway. Do you hear me?"

Lydia looked at the card in shock and dread. Several things were written on it, but the first thing she saw were the letters in bold print saying, "THE ANCHOR ORPHANAGE."

"I-I have to g-go there?" she stammered.

"Yes, that's where you have to go!" her aunt said and shoved the card back into the envelope. "There's money for the train in there, too. I gave you some of my precious money. If you had gone with Mr. Russell, it wouldn't have cost me a cent. It's all your fault, and don't you forget it!"

Lydia did not hear those last words, however. All she could think of was that she was being sent away! Not to the circus, but to an orphanage in a city far away, and she had to go there all by herself! She nervously asked, "Do they know me there? Do they know I'm coming? I-I don't dare."

"Scaredy cat! Coward! You aren't usually so shy. You always act as if you'd dare do anything, but when it comes right down to it, you're a chicken! Now get out of here!" she commanded, pointing to the door. "Out!"

"But do they know me there?" Lydia asked again.

"Yes," Auntie snarled. "You were there for almost two years, and now I wish I had left you there! Now, out!"

Lydia still hesitated. Did she have to leave right now? Couldn't she bring anything along, like clothes and—oh, yes, Papa's letter! She didn't want to leave that behind. It had to go along. She ran from the room and up the steps. The attic was a mess, the closet door was open, and half the contents had fallen out. It was obvious that Aunt Kate had been looking for something. Now Lydia knew it was the card from the orphanage.

Lydia stood uncertainly in the middle of the mess. She didn't have a suitcase, so she couldn't bring any clothes with her. She could only hope the orphanage would give her some clothes. The whole situation was terribly upsetting.

She went to the chest where she kept all her belongings. Auntie had dug around in there, too, but at least Papa's letter was still there, along with her Psalter and Bible. Lydia knew she had to take them along. She also saw Nellie's book, a couple of textbooks from school, some papers, and an old leather pencil case that she had gotten from Nellie.

She was interrupted by a voice from downstairs, calling, "What are you doing up there? Get down here right now, and get out of here!"

Lydia took a final glance around the room. Her eyes filled with tears as she realized she might never see this room or sleep in this bed again.

"Come on!" the shrill voice repeated.

With her Psalter, Bible, and letter in hand, Lydia went downstairs.

Aunt Kate was standing in the hallway, waiting for her. "What were you looking for up there?" she snapped.

"Only these," Lydia replied with a trembling voice. "They're books from school and —"

"I don't care. Here," Auntie said, shoving the envelope into Lydia's hand. Then she disappeared into the living room. Lydia was left to tie her shoelaces alone in the dingy hallway. A tear dropped onto the colorless tiles. Lydia brushed away the tears and tried hard not to cry. She had to be brave. After all, she was ten years old!

She slipped Papa's letter and the two little books into one jacket pocket. Then she folded the yellow envelope and put it into the other pocket. She had to be sure she didn't lose any of them. She tied her scarf around her neck, pulled on her mittens, and was ready to go. Should she say goodbye to her aunts, or should she just leave? Everything was very quiet in the house.

Lydia quietly peeked into the living room. Aunt Kate was standing by the table, and when she heard Lydia, she quickly turned around to look. "Well, what do you know? Aren't you gone yet? Wait, I'll —" but Lydia was gone. The door slammed shut, and Lydia ran down the street. She was on her way to the train station; on her way to the unknown!

Fortunately, Papa's letter was still there.

CHAPTER 6

It was quiet on the platform where Lydia was sitting. She'd found a long wooden bench by a wall and decided to sit down there to wait for her train. As she sat, she watched a man who was driving a flatbed wagon stacked with boxes. He was a friendly man, and he stopped to talk to her now and then. She asked him what train she should take and what time it would arrive.

"Well, young lady," he replied, "if you had been here five minutes ago, you could have caught the last one. Now you'll have to be patient. Another train is coming at twelve-oh-eight. I'll let you know when it gets here." Then he asked her whether she were going somewhere to visit. Lydia nodded but didn't say anything else. She didn't want to tell him everything.

If it weren't for the upsetting circumstances that had caused her trip, Lydia would have been enjoying herself. As she bought her ticket at the ticket counter, she felt quite important to be traveling all alone.

"Round-trip or one-way?" the man asked.

"One-way, please," Lydia replied, acting as if she took the train every day. She thought a one-way ticket would be expensive enough, and she didn't want to spend all her money on the ticket. She hadn't had any idea it would cost so much. Her aunt must have known, though, because she had given Lydia just enough money to cover the ticket and leave a little change for her to use later.

Lydia saw a train coming and noticed that it was a long one. As it came to a stop, passengers streamed off. Some of the people had suitcases, and there were a couple of soldiers. Most of the people seemed to be in a hurry, but Lydia noticed one who stopped and looked around while searching the faces.

It was interesting to watch everything. Lydia couldn't remember ever riding on a train before, but she was enjoying the experience so far. She watched as a heavy-set lady ran by, and she thought the lady was probably worried she'd miss her train. On the other side of the platform another train had stopped. This was a really busy place, with people running in all directions.

There was a loud whistle, and one of the trains left the station. Then an announcement told the passengers not to stand close to the rails because a train would be passing through from Brussels. Lydia could see it coming in the distance, and within moments the train raced past the platform. She held her breath as it sped by, and her eyes opened wide as she watched it disappear.

"You think that's fast?" asked the jolly voice of the man driving the luggage cart.

"Of course! Don't you?" Lydia responded.

"Oh, no, that's not fast!" the man laughed.

"You mean they all go that fast?" Lydia asked curiously.

"Sure. What do you think? The train you're going to take goes even faster! Did you ever hear of the hovercraft that travels from Calais to Dover? Never heard of it? Well, it's a type of boat that skims over the water. It actually seems to fly over the water. Your train goes like that, too. Not over the water, of course, but over the rails. It goes so fast that it actually glides."

Lydia laughed. "I don't believe it. I've never seen such a thing!"

"So you don't believe me? Just wait. When you're sitting in the train, you'll know what I mean." The man drove off, whistling.

******

Once more, it was quiet on the platform. Lydia looked at the big clock and saw that it was almost eleven-thirty. The time had flown by! Her train would be coming in a few minutes. She wondered if she would enjoy her ride and how long it would take. She also worried about how she would know where she had to get off. What if she got off at the wrong stop? She decided to ask the man when he came back again.

More people were arriving on the platform now, and Lydia wondered if they were going to take the same train she was taking. She looked nervously at the door through which the man usually came, hoping she would have a chance to see him before the train came! Finally she saw him, without his cart this time. He was talking with a man and woman.

Lydia stood up. The man kept talking to the couple, and Lydia wondered if she should interrupt him since the train could be arriving at any time. Suddenly he looked in her direction and said something to the couple, and then they looked her way, too. Lydia quickly turned her head away. He had probably said something about her, or they wouldn't have all looked at her.

She saw another train approaching and realized it had to be hers. Now she was becoming more nervous. The whole situation was all so strange. She had never traveled before, and now she was going somewhere all alone. She looked toward the man again and was relieved to see him coming toward her, but the people with whom he had been talking were coming with him.

"Young lady," he said, "here are a couple of travel companions for you. You get off the train one station before they do, so they can keep you company the whole way!"

The woman nodded in a friendly way, and the man said, "Sure, we'll keep an eye on you."

"Yes, because she is a daring young lady! She doesn't believe what an old man tells her about trains. Boys, you believe me, don't you?" and he began telling the same story to the boys who were with the man and woman.

The oldest one exclaimed, "No way, that's not true! There's no such train."

"So, you don't believe me either? How terrible! Well, friends, I would say it's time to get on the train before it leaves without you. Have a good trip, everyone! And children, don't get sick, because that happens easily in those fast trains." Laughing heartily, he walked away.

"Martin, you carry this suitcase, and Ritchie, stay by Mama," their father directed. Then he picked up a little boy who looked about three years old and carried him.

"Come on," said the woman to Lydia, as they walked across the platform. "It's quieter inside." They all boarded the train and walked down the aisle a little way before selecting their seats.

Martin and Ritchie quickly slid over to the window.

"Do you want to sit by the window, too?" the man asked Lydia.

"It doesn't matter, sir," she replied.

"Then you go sit next to Ritchie," he instructed.

The woman sat down across from Lydia, next to Martin, while the man and the little boy sat on the bench across the aisle. Across from him sat a portly man with a newspaper spread out in front of him, just as if he were at home.

"What's your name?" the woman asked Lydia.

"Lydia, ma'am."

"That's a pretty name."

"From the Bible," Ritchie said, "from the story about Paul. Our teacher told us about it."

"Exactly. You're a good listener."

The little boy slid off the bench and went to his mother.

"I want to sit with you," he said, looking at Lydia with his big dark eyes as he went to sit across from her.

"That's Lydia," his mother said. "Tell her what your name is."

"Peter de Graaf, 17 Main Street," he replied proudly, and they all laughed.

Then they heard the train whistle blowing. "We're on our way," the boys called out, and they pressed their noses against the window. Soon they were moving, and they all looked out the windows. The train gained speed, but Lydia was sure it wasn't as fast as the train from Brussels.

For a while everyone was quiet except for Martin, who exclaimed now and then, "Look at that!" Before long, though, the children were tired of looking outside, since they often traveled by train.

"Do you always travel alone?" Martin asked Lydia.

"Well, I never take the train," she answered.

"I would dare to go alone," Ritchie piped up.

"Dare to? The problem is that it's no fun to go alone. I have traveled alone so often!" Martin boasted.

"Yes, but you are older than Ritchie, Martin. When you were eight years old, I did not permit you to go alone either," his mother said.

Then it was quiet again, until Peter suddenly said, "Mama! I don't want to ride on the train anymore."

"You don't? Well, then I'll let you off the train pretty soon, okay? And we'll go on without you," she teased.

"Really, Mama?" Ritchie asked, taking her seriously.

"No, Ritchie. Peter will stay right here with us. Right, Peter?" Mother gave her little boy a hug.

Nice little boys, Lydia thought, and their mother seemed friendly, too. Imagine what it would be like if she would say to Lydia, "You may come along with us and stay in our home." How wonderful that would be! Then she wouldn't have to go to the orphanage.

Lydia tried not to think about it. She kept brushing the thought away, and she listened to the cheerful chatter of the boys instead. Meanwhile, the train chugged along the tracks, bringing her closer to her destination. Soon she would have to step out of the train and then....

"Hey, don't you hear me? I asked if you were going somewhere on a visit." Martin's voice startled Lydia.

"On a visit? No...um...I'm going...well...." She got no farther.

"Oh, you're going home," Martin concluded, and Lydia left it at that.

"Do you have any little brothers or sisters, Lydia?" Mrs. De Graaf asked.

"No, ma'am," Lydia answered.

"If you are an only child, you must be spoiled. That always happens. Joanne van der Vlis in my class is, too," Martin said.

"A little indulging doesn't hurt," his mother observed. "I think Lydia would really like to have a little brother or sister, too."

Meanwhile, the train had stopped. "What a small platform," Martin said loudly. No one was boarding the train here.

"It is very quiet," the portly man with the newspaper said. He folded his paper and started up a conversation with Mr. De Graaf. The train stayed at the station only for a moment before continuing on.

Peter got up and started walking through the train car, looking around him as he went. Martin, who had had enough sitting, stood up, too, but his mother said, "Stay here, Martin, or you'll get yourself into trouble."

"But I'm getting awfully tired of sitting."

The portly man heard this.

"Those rascals! I can understand that sitting still gets tiring after a while. When I was young, I couldn't sit still for long either." He chuckled. "If I sat still for five minutes, it was because I was thinking up some mischief!"

"So, you were a naughty boy once, too," Mr. De Graaf said, laughing.

"That's right!" He chuckled again, "And my wife says I still am sometimes. Yes, sir, we were just talking about a chance of snow soon. Well, I hope so, especially for those little rascals. Once in a while my hat gets knocked off by a snowball, but I can't get angry about it. I used to throw a few snowballs myself. I wouldn't mind trying it again, but I can't run as fast as I used to! Besides, it looks a bit strange for a heavy-set old man like me to be throwing snowballs." He laughed at his own joke.

The children laughed along with him. They could just picture him throwing snowballs!

The conversation was interrupted for a bit while the conductor came around to punch their tickets. The jolly old man tried to chat with him, but the conductor looked very unfriendly and said nothing. "He must have gotten out of the wrong side of bed this morning," the man grumbled after the conductor had gone.

The train was now traveling past some desolate pastureland. The sky, which had been a beautiful clear blue, was now becoming gray. It looked as if it might snow.

"Is it almost my stop?" Lydia asked Mrs. De Graaf.

"Let's see. It's one-oh-five. Another forty-five minutes, I think. Are you getting tired of riding, too?"

Lydia was not at all tired of the ride. She would have liked to stay on the train much longer. The train was bringing her closer and closer to the orphanage, and when she thought about that, she felt very uneasy.

If it weren't for these friendly, cheerful people, she would feel very lonely. They didn't know that she had been sent away. In fact, they really didn't know much of anything about her.

******

Mrs. De Graaf looked at the girl across from her. A strange girl, she thought. Lydia was getting along very well with the boys, but at the same time she looked troubled, as if she were thinking about something very upsetting. How could such a young girl already have unhappiness in her life?

When Martin had asked her whether she were going for a visit, she had looked shocked and had given him a very strange answer. It was obvious that something was bothering the girl. Besides, she looked a little neglected with her faded blue coat. After all, it was Christmas time, when she should have been wearing her best clothes. Maybe this girl didn't have any good clothes. The woman didn't know where her traveling companion had come from. Maybe she came from a poor family, she thought. The girl was very polite, and she talked decently.

Lydia blushed when she sensed that her neighbor was studying her, but Mrs. De Graaf gave her a friendly smile and pulled a couple of chocolate bars out of her purse. "Boys, who would like some chocolate?" she called to them.

Well, no one could refuse that! "We'll have to divide them or I won't have enough," she warned. "Sir, would you like one, too?" she asked the heavy-set man.

"Would I like chocolate? Certainly! It's not good for me, but half a bar now and then won't hurt me. He chuckled loudly. Then everyone was quiet as they enjoyed their pieces of chocolate.

The portly gentleman looked at his watch. "In twenty minutes I'll be there. I've made this trip quite a few times, sometimes three or four times a week. My wife is in a hospital that specializes in eye problems, but she's improving now. Last week the doctor told me, "Boom, if all goes well, your wife will be home before New Year's."

After talking together for a while Mr. Boom announced, "I had an enjoyable time and here's my stop already. Have a good trip.

The children looked out the train window, and waved goodbye to Mr. Boom.

******

The rest of the train ride went smoothly. The children talked about school for a while, but Lydia became quieter and quieter. She knew she was getting closer to the orphanage, and she wondered whether it would be far from the station. If it were, how would she get there? She was glad her thoughts were constantly interrupted by Martin's jolly chatter. "What class are you in?" he asked.

"Fifth grade."

"I am, too. We have a very nice teacher, much nicer than the one in fourth grade. There we couldn't do anything, and the teacher never smiled. It was no fun. If we wiggled a little bit, he gave us extra work."

"Yes, my boy," his mother said with a smile, "and now that you are in that 'nice' teacher's class, you never get extra work, right?" and she looked at him teasingly.

"Well, only a couple of times, but that was by accident," Martin said, trying to defend himself. "Does your father always think you have homework because you were naughty in school, too?" he asked, looking at Lydia.

"I…I don't have a father," Lydia replied softly.

"Oh." Martin's face turned red, and he quickly looked out the window.

"That is too bad, child," his mother said, "to be so young and not have a father."

Lydia nodded. It was quiet for a moment.

Solemnly Ritchie looked at Lydia. How sad not to have a father. If he didn't have a father, it would be terrible. At least she must have a loving mother. To comfort her, he said at once, "You have a dear mother, don't you?"

Then Lydia said softly, "I don't have a mother either."

The boys were shocked. No father *and* no mother. How terrible!

"Do you live all alone?" Ritchie asked. He couldn't get over something so horrible.

"No, of course not," came a sharp reply from Mrs. De Graaf, who sensed that Lydia didn't want to talk about it. How pitiful. Such a young child without a father or a mother.

"You are a brave girl," she said at once, sounding very sympathetic and kind. It almost made Lydia feel like crying.

Then Ritchie added, "I…I think you are sweet, Lydia. If…if I did not have a father and mother, I would cry all the time, and…."

But Martin stood up and grumbled, "Don't be so silly!" and went to sit by his father. He couldn't stand it when everyone talked so seriously. That know-it-all Ritchie, he thought, had better be quiet.

In the meantime, Peter was looking for some attention. He was wide awake now and said, "I want to sit there," and he quickly climbed onto Martin's seat. "All boats," he cried, and Ritchie, who loved boats, pressed his nose against the window.

"Look at that big one. It's too bad we're past it already."

Mrs. De Graaf was glad that Ritchie's attention had been drawn to something else. The boy was very sensitive, and sometimes he could talk on and on about serious things. He meant well. He always wanted to comfort people, but he was still young and didn't realize that sometimes it was better to say nothing when someone was feeling sad. If Lydia's father and mother had died recently, reminding her might make her cry.

Mrs. De Graaf took a roll of peppermints from her purse and passed them around. "You must be getting hungry from such a long ride," she said, smiling at Lydia. "It won't be long now, though."

When they reached the next station, some soldiers entered the train, talking noisily. Two of them went to sit by Mr. De Graaf and Martin, which the boys thought was wonderful. How exciting to be a soldier! Before long, Martin began asking hundreds of questions. "Do you ever have to fight? Do you really shoot your guns?" The questions followed one right after another. The soldiers patiently answered each one, while everyone listened.

Finally, they had almost reached the station where Lydia would have to get off. "You are almost there, Lydia," Mrs. De Graaf informed her. "You don't have a suitcase with you, do you? Be careful, won't you? It is very busy here."

"Too bad you have to get out here," Ritchie observed.

When the train came to a stop, Lydia stood up. Mrs. De Graaf rummaged in her purse and pressed something into Lydia's hand. A dollar!

"Oh, thank you very much," Lydia said, surprised. A dollar all for herself! How nice!

"Well, child, we wish you the best, and we enjoyed traveling with you." Mrs. De Graaf said, while Ritchie nodded vigorously in agreement.

"Goodbye!" they all called.

"Bye!" Lydia responded.

They warmly exchanged good wishes as if they had known each other for years. As Lydia stepped off the train, she heard Peter's voice asking, "Why is Lydia going away now?" She thought he was such a sweet boy! They were all very friendly, and now she would never see them again. Too bad!

As she stood on the station platform, Lydia's eyes searched the windows of the train. There they were. They waved, and Lydia waved back. Then she turned and looked around for the exit. It was very different here from the other station platform where she had started her journey. This one was much bigger and much busier. Feeling a bit lost, Lydia walked through the crowd of people. She saw buses, cars, and people all around her. What now? Where should she go? She was a lonely girl in a big city—a lonely girl who didn't know her way around in this big city. Who would help her? Then, right there on that busy street, among all those people, a sigh came into her heart, "Lord, help me. I don't know where I should go. Help me!"

No one else knew that, though, and no one heard it. No one? Yes, the Lord, a Father of the fatherless, knows everything and hears everything, and He could help!

CHAPTER 7

Lydia pulled the card from her bag to see where the orphanage was—205 Rembrandt Lane. First, she was going to have to ask someone where that was.

"Sir, do you know where Rembrandt Lane is?" she asked a man standing at a bus stop.

"No, I'm not familiar with this area. You should ask one of the bus drivers."

Across the street were two empty buses. Lydia saw the drivers standing next to them, talking together, so she decided to go over and ask them.

"Do you know where Rembrandt Lane is?"

"Rembrandt Lane? Yes, I do. You have to take Line 4A, and then transfer to Line 5 at Dam Square," one driver answered.

"Look," the other driver said, pointing, "Line 4A stops there, and it should be here any time. You can ride to the end of the line."

Lydia did not have to wait long before the bus came. The ticket cost forty-five cents. Fortunately, the lady on the train had given her a dollar, so she had some money left in case she had to take another bus. Just to be sure, she told the bus driver that she had to go to Rembrandt Lane.

"This bus goes to Dam Square, and you have to transfer when you get there," he said.

The ride would take at least half an hour. Lydia was amazed at how big the city was, filled with big buildings and broad streets. Her city was small compared to this one.

Her city? No, she couldn't call the city where her aunts lived *her* city anymore. From now on this one would be hers.

When Lydia thought about the orphanage, her heart beat faster. She was getting closer and closer, and she still didn't know what she would say when she got there. Should she just say, "I am Lydia van Arkel, and I'm coming here to live"?

No, she couldn't say that, but maybe they would still remember her. How long had it been? She was ten years old now. How long would she have stayed in the orphanage? Until she was three? It couldn't have been much longer, or she would have remembered something about it. She guessed it had probably been about seven years ago. Well, maybe if she told them her name, they would remember her, unless someone else had taken over the orphanage.

Many children would be there, and Lydia wondered what they were doing right now. Maybe they were celebrating Christmas. What would they think if she walked in during their Christmas celebration? That might be awkward, and Lydia worried they might say, "What are you doing here? You don't belong here!"

On the other hand, there was always the possibility they would be very friendly. She had often asked the Lord if He would change the circumstances in her life, and anything was possible with Him. He could make all things well.

When Lydia thought about this, she was filled with wonder, as if the Lord Jesus was close to her. It was as if He said, "Lydia, be not afraid. I came down to earth and was forsaken by everyone, even My heavenly Father, in order to make people truly happy again. I will not leave you alone!"

Although Lydia still felt lonely in that big, unknown city, she also had a feeling of joy that was wonderful!

The bus stopped again. This time they were at Dam Square, and all the passengers got out. Before getting off, Lydia asked the driver again where Line 5 stopped.

"Over there by the furniture store," he replied.

What a huge square! It seemed as if everything in this city was big. She had to cross to the other side of the square to catch her bus. She saw a bus coming, so she ran to catch it. Yes, it was Line 5. She waved at the driver, and, thankfully, he saw her.

"You're just in time," he said. "I was ready to keep on going because no one was waiting. I'll be glad for some company, since it's been pretty quiet today. Are you going to Rembrandt Lane? Oh, that's not very far, hardly worth riding there!"

If Lydia had known that it was such a short distance, she would have walked. Now she was out forty-five cents. Oh, well, she still had sixty cents left. She had never been so rich. She would have to make sure she didn't lose it.

"What number do you need?" the driver asked.

Lydia took out the card and looked at it again.

"Number 205? That's behind some other buildings. I'll be turning onto Vermeer Street soon, and that's the best place to get off. Are you familiar with the area?"

"No, not at all," Lydia replied.

"That's what I thought, but we'll get you there, okay?" assured the driver.

They drove over a bridge, turned left, and then stopped at an intersection. "I have to turn onto this side street, but you should keep going straight. See, the odd-numbered buildings are on the other side of the street. You have quite a walk before you get to number 205." Lydia stepped off the bus, waited until he had gone past, and then crossed the street.

It was a very wide street, with tall trees on both sides. Lydia thought it was a pleasant street, and she really liked the grand houses! Would the orphanage be as big and stately, too? She hoped it would be.

Let's see. Here was number 75. She still had a long way to go, so Lydia started walking faster. The sun had completely disappeared behind thick gray clouds, and the wind was picking up, but Lydia didn't notice. She thought about only one thing: the orphanage! When she was past number 171, she started slowing down. She was almost there.

She looked down the street. On one side of the street were all individual houses that were large and quite stately. On the other side, the houses were all attached to each other and looked alike. They were nice, too, but they weren't nearly as attractive.

The orphanage must be close to the end of the street. Oh, how scary! Lydia hardly dared to go farther. She hoped the people would be friendly and would remember her. But what if there were no room for her? Maybe the orphanage was full!

She wondered what the children would be like. Maybe they wouldn't like it that a stranger was joining them. Maybe.... Number 195, 197. She was almost there.

******

Lydia's eyes moved along the houses. There. It had to be that one! She was looking at a big white house standing a little way back from the others. She saw no one, no children, nothing. In front of all the windows hung long white curtains.

Her heart pounded as she stood by the gate, and her eyes searched the front of the house. The whole place looked very desolate. Could this be The Anchor? She didn't see a sign anywhere. How strange. Wait! There on the left was a post with a sign saying, W. C. L. Voorthuizen, physician.

Wide-eyed, she stared at the sign. How could that be? This was number 205. The orphanage had to be right here. Could she be mistaken about the number? She pulled out the card again. Yes, it was 205.

She looked around uncertainly. Now what should she do? Then it occurred to her that the numbers may have been changed. That happened sometimes.

She decided to walk up and down the street and look carefully at each house. Hopefully she would find it that way. But after she had walked down the whole street, she still hadn't found The Anchor.

There she stood, all alone in a strange city. It was very quiet. The only sound came from the howling of the wind. It was a sharp northeast wind, but Lydia didn't even notice it. She was too concerned about finding the orphanage.

Suddenly she wondered if she might have ended up on the wrong street. The bus driver had said this was Rembrandt Lane, but he could have been mistaken. Again her eyes searched along the houses. Finally she saw a sign with a street name on it. It said, Rembrandt Lane! She was in the right place. Everything was there: the street, the number, but not the orphanage.

Discouraged, Lydia walked back to where she had started. She would take another good look. If she didn't find it this time, she would have to ask someone.

A little later she was standing in front of number 205 again, the doctor's house. She debated whether or not to ring the doorbell, but everything looked so forsaken. No one seemed to be home.

All of a sudden, she heard a woman's voice calling, "Hector, come here!"

Lydia quickly turned around to look. On the other side of the street, she saw a woman standing by a car, calling her dog. She decided to ask that lady about the orphanage and ran across the street.

"Ma'am, do you know where the orphanage, The Anchor, is?" she asked, and then waited anxiously for the woman's answer.

"Orphanage? The Anchor?" she asked, thinking. "No, I've never heard of it. Is it supposed to be here?"

"Yes," Lydia replied, "at 205 Rembrandt Lane."

"Rembrandt Lane, number 205?" the woman asked, puzzled. "Number 205 is on that side of the street, but there is no orphanage there. I just moved here, though. Why don't you ask someone at number 178? Those people have lived there for forty-five years. They should know."

Off Lydia went again. She walked down the street to number 178 and turned into the small yard. As the gate closed behind her, she saw an elderly man sitting by a window, looking out. When he saw her, he stood up. She didn't even have to ring the doorbell. Soon the door opened, and the friendly old man looked at her questioningly.

"Sir, do you know where the orphanage, The Anchor, is?" Lydia asked.

It was quiet for a moment. Then he guardedly replied, "The Anchor? Why, our house faced it for thirty-seven or thirty-eight years. First, it was a home for skippers' children. That's where the name, The Anchor, came from. When it became empty, it was used for a couple of years as an orphanage. I remember it as clearly as if it were yesterday. I went there almost every day because I delivered bread to them, you see. There were about forty children."

Lydia listened impatiently to the whole story. Finally, even though it wasn't very polite, she interrupted him. "Yes, but where is the orphanage now? I can't find it anywhere."

"Where is it? Well, it hasn't been there for about seven years. There were all kinds of problems, you see. The building has been torn down. In fact, all the houses on the other side of the street have been demolished. They have really improved that side of the street. Look at what they've built instead!" He proudly pointed in that direction, but Lydia wasn't interested and didn't even hear the rest of what he said. The man's words resounded in her ears. "Torn down…demolished…." She blinked her eyes and swallowed hard.

The old man didn't notice and kept on talking, until Lydia interrupted again and asked with a trembling voice, "But where are the children?"

The friendly old man looked at her questioningly.

"What children? Oh, you mean the orphans? Well, one was sent here and another there, you understand. It's unfortunate because, after all, they were poor wretches who had no mothers or fathers anymore. Too bad!"

Suddenly his wife interrupted and called to him, "Carl, what are you doing out there talking so long? Do you want to catch a cold? Close the door!"

"Yes, I'm coming. Well, young lady, now you know. I wish you the best," he said, and with a friendly nod, he closed the door.

Lydia stayed standing there for a moment. She didn't know what to do next. No orphanage! What now? She was startled when the front door opened again.

"I'm sorry I just left you standing there. You asked about the orphanage. Do you need to go there?" The old man standing in the doorway, now with a thick wool scarf around his neck, looked at her curiously.

Lydia nodded. "Yes, sir."

"Are you on an errand? Or do you have to speak with someone?"

"Uh…no…or…well, yes," she said, and then she ran out of the tiny yard and down the street. The old man watched her in astonishment and shook his head.

"She just left me standing here," he mumbled. "How nice. Kids these days!" he exclaimed and then shut the door, since a cold wind was blowing in. Brrr! It was not a good day to be outside. It was much better inside by the glowing red coals in the stove.

******

Lydia kept running. She was on her way to the station. There was no other choice but to go back to her aunts' house. What else could she do? She had completely forgotten that she didn't have any money left for the train.

She had to go to the big Dam Square where she would catch the bus to the train station. She remembered the way: down Rembrandt Lane to the crossroads. So far, so good. See, around that corner was the bridge. Now down that narrow street, which she remembered taking before. Oh, yes, she knew where to go. Panting a little from running, she reached Dam Square. Which bus line should she take? A long line of people were waiting by one of the stops.

Lydia approached a lady standing at the end of the line and asked which bus went to the station.

"This bus goes to the station," she said.

So Lydia decided to take that bus. She didn't have long to wait. More people who had to take that bus were coming out of a building. What a busy place!

Lydia quickly took two quarters out of her jacket pocket. The bus driver handed her a ticket, and Lydia waited for the five-cents change. Didn't it cost forty-five cents?

The bus driver, however, looked away and helped someone else. She had to keep walking whether she liked it or not, for she was pushed along by the people who were behind her. She didn't dare say anything, but she thought it was mean, very mean!

Although the bus was very full, she managed to find a place to sit. She knew she had to watch carefully where the bus went, but it would be quite a while before they reached the station. It was too bad she wasn't sitting by a window, but she saw that they were on a wide street, just like when she came. She concluded that she must be on the right bus.

After about twenty minutes, quite a few people had gotten off the bus. The boy next to her got off, too, so Lydia slid over by the window. The streets they were taking now didn't look familiar to her, but she figured she must have forgotten some of them.

Then she heard someone say, "We are approaching the end of the line." When the bus stopped, all the other people stepped out. The driver stood up and looked back through the bus.

"Out," he said gruffly when he saw Lydia. "You have to get out!"

Lydia stood up and said, "But I have to go to the train station!"

The driver didn't listen and said again, "You have to get out."

Lydia obeyed, but she didn't understand. Wasn't the train station here? A whole row of buses were standing there, but she didn't see the station.

She had to ask someone again. She looked around and saw a man standing by a gas pump. She went to him and asked, "Where is the station, sir?"

"The station? You're standing right in front of it. Or do you mean the train station? Oh, you want to catch a train. Then you are nowhere close. You will have to take Line 7."

Lydia was startled to hear that she should have taken a different bus.

"How…how far is it to walk to the train station?" she asked fearfully.

"I think about forty-five minutes."

Discouraged, Lydia looked around. Did she have to go back on the bus? But she didn't have enough money!

She wanted to ask the man something else, but just then he walked away with another man. Lydia felt like crying. What should she do? She wanted to go home, home to her aunts, away from this horrible big city.

It was already dusk, and soon it would be dark. The evening would become night, and no one would be left on the streets. It was very cold. The wind pulled at her jacket as if to say, "Get out of here, you don't belong here." Lydia became more and more afraid. Then, without asking anyone which way she had to go, she began to run again. She had to get home, and quickly, before it got dark. She just kept running—running in the wrong direction. She didn't think about that. She thought only about going home. But how would she get there? It was so far! And she had only one dime left.

CHAPTER 8

It was evening. The wind was howling through the streets, and from time to time there was a heavy shower of hail on the pavement. Once in a while, a car appeared on the deserted streets, but otherwise everything was very still. Nobody wanted to venture out in this weather.

Inside by the warm stove, it was cozy, even though the wind lashed and the hail struck sharply against the window. It was not wise to be outside on this day after Christmas. It was dark outside, dark and cold.

But who was that trudging down the street? Who dared to brave the cold, dark evening and the wild gusts of wind?

It was Lydia. Lydia was still walking, still determined to reach her aunts! She was very tired and terribly cold. She had thrust her hands deep into her pockets, and she had tied her hood tightly around her face. It didn't help much, for the wind found its way through everything.

Suddenly the hailstorm increased, and the sharp stones struck against her face. Lydia was forced to look for shelter whenever the hail came down too hard. When she couldn't find any shelter, she had no choice but to keep walking. Sometimes, when the wind was too strong for her, she had to stand still and wait for it to let up.

For a long time she wandered through the big, strange city. As it grew darker outside, lights started to blink on in the houses. Lydia looked at them longingly. Once, as she passed a house, she heard singing. When she stopped and looked inside, the scene was very inviting. A couple of candles were burning, and in a corner of the room stood a big Christmas tree full of lights. But the nicest sight of all was next to the tree. Children were standing by an organ, singing. Lydia could hear them clearly over the noise of the wind, and it sounded beautiful to her. She remembered the hymn from school.

Silent night, holy night!
All is calm, all is bright
Round yon virgin, mother and Child,
Holy Infant, so tender and mild,
Sleep in heavenly peace,
Sleep in heavenly peace.

Then the children sang:

O little town of Bethlehem
how still we see thee lie!
Above thy deep and dreamless sleep
the silent stars go by;
Yet in thy dark streets shineth
the everlasting light;
The hopes and fears of all the years
are met in thee tonight.

As Lydia stood listening, she didn't feel the cold anymore. She only heard the lovely singing and saw the children around the organ. Then, suddenly, a woman stood by the window. She looked angrily at Lydia, and with a jerk she pulled the drapes closed as if to say, "Go away, nosy girl. Mind your own business. We are celebrating Christmas."

Lydia quickly ran away from there. She felt like crying. The singing had been so nice, and she had forgotten all her troubles for a little while. Then the woman had made it clear that Lydia did not belong there, and that made her feel even lonelier than before.

Everyone else was celebrating Christmas, but she was walking outside in the dark and cold. She belonged to no one, and no one was thinking about her. Nobody cared about her.

Oh, if only she had not been sent away. If only everything had been a dream, and she would wake up in the old, familiar attic room, safe and warm under the blankets. For the first time in her life, Lydia longed for the little house on the quiet, dreary street. Even if Aunt Trudy never said anything to her and Aunt Kate always complained, she wouldn't care. If only she were back home! She would never be dissatisfied again.

She wondered if she would ever be able to find her aunts' house again. It was so far to walk, and she didn't even know whether she was walking in the right direction. She was completely lost, and it was almost night. Lydia became even more afraid. She wanted to run faster, but she couldn't. She was too tired.

When she came to a quiet street, she sat down in the cold, wet grass and leaned against a tree. As she pressed her head against the rough bark, she whimpered in a soft, helpless voice, "Papa, Mama." The words sounded good to her ears. She had never been able to call anyone Papa or Mama, but now it sounded pathetic and sorrowful. There was no one to hear her.

Everyone else was celebrating Christmas. Children were gathered together singing:

Away in a manger, no crib for His bed,
The little Lord Jesus lay down His sweet head.
The stars in the sky look down where He lay,
The little Lord Jesus, asleep on the hay.

The Lord lived high in the heavens, and He looked down on the earth. Was there a place for the Lord Jesus today? On this day after Christmas, when thousands of people were singing about Him? Who was really calling to Him?

On that quiet street, an exhausted little girl leaned against a rough, wet tree, not knowing what she should do anymore. She had called out to her father and mother, but they couldn't help her. But there was another Father, and in Lydia's heart she cried to Him, "Lord, help me. Please help me, for Jesus' sake."

It was dark, very dark, and still and cold.

Then the lonely girl clearly heard:

He had such love for sinners that He died for them.

Who was singing that? Where was it coming from? She was too far away from the children to hear them singing anymore. She couldn't understand it, but those lines were very comforting. If the Lord Jesus would love her, wouldn't she be truly blessed? And couldn't the Lord Jesus understand, who Himself was so poor and forsaken in this dark world? Yes, He could certainly hear her. The Lord was able to help her.

Papa himself had written, "He is a Father of the fatherless!"

CHAPTER 9

It was quiet in the parsonage. Three people sat in the cozy living room, quietly reading: Reverend Vermeulen, his wife, and his aged mother, who lived with them. The ticking of a clock and the occasional turning of a page were the only sounds to be heard. Otherwise the room was very still.

Mrs. Vermeulen looked at the clock. It was only seven-thirty, so she decided to wait before preparing coffee.

It was so nice and peaceful, she thought, and it felt good to be able to sit down and relax together. She hoped it would stay that way. A nice, quiet evening would do her husband good. He was always very busy and often had to go away at night. She was glad he could be home this evening, the day after Christmas. She hoped that for once no one would come to the door to ask for him.

Hail beat sharply against the windows, and the wind howled around the house. Grandma looked up. "Oh, what terrible weather. It wouldn't be any fun to be outdoors tonight," she said and slid her chair closer to the stove.

"Shall I close the drapes?" Mrs. Vermeulen asked. "It will keep the heat in, and there's nothing to see out there anyway."

She stood up to close them, but the minister absentmindedly said, "Oh, leave them open for a while."

A little puzzled, his wife looked at him, sat down again, and picked up her book, but she didn't read. Now and then she looked at her husband and noticed that he wasn't really reading either. He was very quiet tonight. She had observed that at suppertime already.

That afternoon he had preached in a village not far from their town. As usual, she had asked him about it, but he had answered her very distractedly. Both she and Grandma had noticed it, but neither of them had asked him any more questions. They had assumed something must have happened or something was bothering him, and they knew they would just have to wait patiently until he was ready to tell them about it.

"I'm glad it's letting up," Grandma said, meaning the hail and wind. "It's hard to believe the Christmas season is nearly past again. Time flies." Then she bent over her book and continued reading.

******

It was quiet again, both indoors and out. The hail had stopped, and the wind had died down. Suddenly Rev. Vermeulen exclaimed, "That's it! Now I remember!"

Startled, Grandma and Mrs. Vermeulen looked at the minister.

"What do you remember?" his wife asked.

"What do you remember?" Grandma repeated.

"Well, about that girl I saw this afternoon."

Again two responses, "What girl?"

The minister laid his book on the table next to him.

"Let me tell you," he said as he sat back in his chair. "This afternoon, as I was driving home, I had to stop at the main intersection of the Westersingel. It was dark already, but I noticed a young girl leaning against a streetlight. I thought she was waiting for me to cross the intersection, so when she looked at me, I motioned for her to cross first, but she just stood there."

The minister stopped for a moment.

Grandma and Mrs. Vermeulen looked at him expectantly and wondered what was coming next. After all, it wasn't unusual to see a girl waiting somewhere.

Then the minister continued, "She looked at me for a second, but when she saw me motioning to her, she looked the other way. As I continued on my way, I saw her face clearly in the glow of the streetlight. She looked at me again, and I was touched by that look. She looked so helpless. So…well…how should I say it? Well, she looked as if she didn't know where to go. She looked so needy." There was silence again.

"Ahh," Grandma said then. "There is much sadness. Maybe the girl had a boyfriend and is —"

"A boyfriend?" the minister interrupted. "No, she was only about ten years old. That's why it struck me so much. Such a young girl, and it looked as if she had already experienced much grief in her life. That wasn't all, though. It seemed as though I had seen that girl before. She looked so familiar, especially the look in her eyes. I was sure that I knew her.

"I kept thinking and thinking, but I could not remember who she was. I didn't know how I knew her, either, but I could not forget her face. I tried to forget about her, but I kept remembering those big, fearful eyes that seemed to cry out for help. And now, all of a sudden, I know!"

"Oh?" Mrs. Vermeulen asked with interest. "Do I know her, too? Is she someone from our church?"

"No," the minister replied, "I don't know the girl herself, but she looks exactly like someone I knew very well. Do you know who it is? Esther van Arkel."

"Esther van Arkel? Wasn't that the —"

"Yes, the young woman who, with her husband, had an accident in the circus. It was quite a few years ago, but I still remember it well. Things like that are unforgettable."

The minister stared into space, deep in thought.

"That was the year that I was so sick, wasn't it?" Mrs. Vermeulen said.

"Yes, it was. It was a difficult year, but everything turned out so wonderfully. One time when I came to see you in the hospital, I happened to enter the wrong room. It was all meant to be that way, of course. There lay that woman, so sick and so afraid. She looked just like the girl I saw this afternoon. She knew that she was going to die, but she was very afraid of death.

"When she was young, she had gone to Sunday school and learned that there was a God. As she grew older, the world had attracted her, and she left her religious upbringing behind. She wanted a carefree, merry life, and she wanted to be famous! Well, she did become famous, and so did her husband. They did not think about having to die since they were young and healthy. They did not ask for God until God began to ask for them. That's why that accident had to happen." The minister stopped again.

Grandma and Mrs. Vermeulen knew the story already, but they listened attentively.

"Everything is possible with the Lord," Grandma said. "Sunday morning you preached about the angel Gabriel saying to Mary, 'Nothing is impossible with the Lord,' and so it is!"

"Yes, so it is," the minister continued, "and that has proven true with Esther and John. We spoke with each other often, and sometimes I was terribly discouraged. I thought I could change their hearts, but only God could do that! I could only show them the way and tell them that the Lord Jesus came down to earth to save sinners.

"The Lord was willing to bless those words. Although at first they had sought their happiness in the world, later they found their happiness in Him in whom alone true happiness can be found. All their former friends would no longer have anything to do with them. They lost them all, but in their place they received the Lord Jesus as their Friend, and He is a Friend who will never let His people go."

The wind picked up again, and hail rattled against the windows, but the three people sitting there didn't notice.

"But this couple had one concern," the minister continued, "and that was their child. They were worried about what would happen to their little girl after they were gone. When I think back, I am ashamed. I tried to reassure them by saying that the Lord is a Helper of the fatherless, and that He could take care of their daughter even when they were not there for her anymore. That is true, of course, but I also said that I would inquire sometime to see how their daughter was doing.

"After John died, so much happened. We moved here, you were very sick, and Father died, but that shouldn't have changed anything. I never thought about the girl again. I am just like the butler who forgot about Joseph when he was released from prison. Who knows what has happened to her!"

"Did she have any extended family?" Mrs. Vermeulen asked.

"Not much. Each of her parents were an only child. I think John did have an elderly mother living somewhere in Belgium." Again there was silence as all three sat deep in thought, thinking about that poor girl who had been left behind, all alone.

Then the minister pictured the girl leaning against the light post again. He could see her big, fearful eyes—eyes that looked exactly like those of that young woman. Why couldn't he get her out of his mind? Why couldn't he forget her face? He saw so many people every day, but now he kept thinking about an unfamiliar child, one whom he would probably never see again.

"Maybe the child lives in Belgium," Mrs. Vermeulen said, her voice breaking the silence.

"What child?" the minister asked absentmindedly.

"Well, Esther and John's child, the one we were talking about."

"Oh, yes. Who knows? That's very possible," the minister said, not sounding very convinced. Without thinking, he picked up his book again and read a line, "What manner of child shall this be!"

The minister did not remember that this question was once spoken about John the Baptist. For him this question referred to the little girl with big, fearful eyes, and out of his heart came the cry, "Lord, Thou knowest it. What about this child? Help her!"

Again his glance fell on a few lines of the closely printed pages of his book: "Thou hast seen it; for Thou beholdest mischief and spite, to requite it with Thy hand: the poor committeth himself unto Thee; Thou art the helper of the fatherless" (Psalm 10:14).

Those words comforted him. "Yes, Lord, Thou seest it. Thou knowest it! I give it over into Thine hands, Thou Helper of the fatherless!"

CHAPTER 10

Lydia was stiff from the cold and had trouble standing, but she knew she had to get up. She couldn't stay sitting on the side of the road in the cold, wet grass! She could hardly move, though. Her feet felt like lead, and her head was pounding. She felt sick from loneliness and cold, but she had to go on.

She didn't know where to go anymore, but still she kept walking. She didn't dare ask anyone how to get to the train station because she was afraid of what the answer might be. Everything seemed like a horrible dream. The aunts and the attic room all seemed very far away, and she wondered whether she would ever see them again.

She looked down the long, deserted street. It was very quiet except for a tall man walking quickly toward her on the other side of the road. Then the man stopped and glanced around. He looked in Lydia's direction and continued staring at her until she became very afraid. Her first thought was to turn around and run away as fast as she could. She did not want to look at that tall, silent man, but she felt she had to keep an eye on him.

She continued walking, a little more slowly now, and as she drew closer, she found he was still watching her. When he saw her looking in his direction, he reached out his hand and called to her.

Lydia was terribly frightened! Again she wondered whether it would be best to turn around, but she didn't know what she would do if he followed her. It was such a long, deserted street! There weren't very many houses, and such a tall man could easily outrun her. She did not like how he kept staring at her, though. If only she could find someone to run to, but there was no one else around—not even on a bike or in a car.

Her heart pounded with fear, and she forgot how tired she was. She wanted to pass the man as quickly as possible and hoped he wouldn't cross the street.

He stood there talking and pointing, but she couldn't understand what he was saying. When she was almost across from him, she didn't look at him any more but ignored him and walked as swiftly as she could. Panting, she kept going while staring straight ahead. In spite of the bone-chilling cold, she was starting to sweat!

She could sense when she was right across from him. "Don't look, keep walking," she told herself, until she was sure she must have passed him. She took a quick look over her shoulder to see whether he had followed her or not. He hadn't moved! She couldn't tell whether he was still looking at her, but she started running anyway. She wanted to get as far away from that tall stranger as she could.

As she approached an intersection, she noticed on the other side of the street a house with warmly lit windows. The light appeared so inviting to her that she decided to go to the house and ring the doorbell. She would tell them about the frightening man. Once Lydia made that decision, she started across the street, without looking to the left or right.

She was about halfway across when there was a loud squealing of tires. A car skidded toward her, swerved, and just missed her before sliding sideways to a stop a little farther down the road.

Lydia was so frightened that she staggered. Everything started whirling, her legs folded under her, and she collapsed onto the cold, wet pavement.

******

In the parsonage, the three people were still sitting peacefully together. All three had picked up their books again. Were they reading? Or were their thoughts somewhere else?

The clock struck eight, and Mrs. Vermeulen laid her book down. "Come on," she said, "let's have a cup of coffee."

"Yes, let's do that," the minister replied and laid his book down, too.

But as Mrs. Vermeulen stood up to go to the kitchen, all three were startled by the sound of screeching tires. The minister jumped up and hurried to the window. He saw a car sideways in the street, and nearby, what looked like a person lying in the middle of the road.

His wife was now standing next to him, and she asked anxiously, "An accident?"

"Yes," was the minister's short reply, and he hurried from the room.

"Put a coat on if you're going outside," his wife called to him as she followed.

Grandma stood up with difficulty and walked slowly to the window. Her hands were trembling.

"Oh, no, an accident," she said softly. "Is it a bad one? O Lord, let it not be serious," she whispered with a prayer from her heart. Then she leaned against the windowsill with her old, wrinkled hands and peered through the darkness. But she didn't see much. Grandma was very old and couldn't see very well anymore. With a sigh she returned to her place by the stove and waited to hear the outcome.

******

Without following his wife's advice to put on a coat, the minister ran outside. Yes, someone was lying there. A man got out of the car and nervously called out, "I couldn't help it. I really couldn't! She ran right in front of me."

Lydia, who had been stunned for a moment, looked in astonishment around her and started to stand up. At first she couldn't remember what had happened, but then it came back to her. A tall man had been staring at her, and she was running away from him. And then a car had almost hit her.

As she remembered all that had happened, she was horrified to see a man coming toward her. Was he the tall, frightening man? She was just ready to get up and run away when she saw there was another man walking behind the first one.

She heard one of the men say, "I really couldn't help it." They approached until they were standing close to her. With anxious, frightened eyes she looked from one man to the other.

Rev. Vermeulen was standing right by her. He looked at her pale face, and he saw her big fearful eyes. A shock went through him. It was that girl! He knew it for sure. She was the same girl he had seen that afternoon!

"Oh, I'm glad it isn't serious," the man next to him exclaimed in relief. "Well, then I can leave now. I have to be at the train station by ten after eight."

"Go ahead. I will bring her home with me," the minister replied. Then he turned to Lydia. "Come on, it's dangerous standing here in the street. Here comes another car," he said and gently nudged Lydia in the direction of his house.

The driver of the car walked away. He was relieved that everything had turned out well, and he was more than happy to let the other man take care of the girl. Feeling free of guilt, he drove off.

"Well, young lady, come inside for a while and catch your breath. Are you hurt?" the minister asked as they made their way up the path to the front door.

Lydia did not answer him. She was terribly frightened, and she was still reeling from all that had happened in the last few minutes.

Mrs. Vermeulen was waiting in the doorway as they approached. "Ah, child," she said, "we are so thankful that you are not hurt. Come inside quickly. Look, your jacket is covered with mud. Take it off, and I will wash it."

Lydia stood in the big, beautiful entryway and blinked her eyes as she looked around.

"Wait, I'll help you." Mrs. Vermeulen's voice sounded welcoming as she bent down to help Lydia unbutton her coat.

"You are so cold and wet," she exclaimed. "Come and warm yourself by the woodstove in the living room." The minister silently watched as his wife helped the girl.

What a sweet girl, Mrs. Vermeulen thought. Who would let such a child wander the streets alone in the dark? "If you will bring her to the living room, I will clean up her coat," she said to her husband.

"Sure. Come along with me," he invited Lydia.

They stepped into the warm, cozy living room, where the lamps spread their friendly light and the stove glowed warmly.

Grandma gazed anxiously at Lydia. “Ah, is it a child?” she asked compassionately. “Is she all right?”

“Yes, fortunately she is. Look, young lady, if you come and sit by the stove, you’ll soon be warm,” the minister said and motioned toward a big chair.

All this time Lydia had not said a word. It all seemed as if she were having a dream that was never going to end.

“Oh, look, your knee is bleeding,” Grandma noticed from her seat across from Lydia.

“I’ll get something to wash it up,” the minister said.

Mrs. Vermeulen came into the room again. “Let me see it. Oh, it’s just skinned a little,” she said and washed Lydia’s knee with a washcloth and put some ointment on it. “Are you hurt anywhere else?”

Lydia shook her blond curls. Now that she was sitting close to the warm stove, her hands and feet felt very strange. She looked up helplessly for a minute, and again the minister was touched by that look. The Lord must no doubt have a certain purpose with this turn of events, he thought, but who was this slender, blond child?

Mrs. Vermeulen left the room again and returned with a glass.

“Here, child, drink this,” she said, handing Lydia the glass.

Lydia took a sip. Her teeth chattered against the glass. Then suddenly Lydia pushed the glass away and began to cry.

“She’s in shock,” Grandma explained.

Mrs. Vermeulen set the glass on a table and laid her hand on Lydia's blond head. "Shhh. It's okay. Everything turned out okay. My husband will bring you home shortly in the car," she said comfortingly.

Lydia hardly heard the word "home." Home sounded so far away. Where was her home? She didn't even have a home.

Three grown people gazed at the weeping girl sitting in the big chair. It was quiet for a moment. Only soft snuffling was heard, and the peaceful ticking of the big clock.

The minister thought, "Lord, Thou seest everything. Thou knowest everything and art a Helper of the fatherless."

He went to the weeping girl, looked at his wife who was trying to comfort her, and said softly, "Let me talk to her."

He sat on the arm of Lydia's chair, laid his arm around her shoulders, and asked, "What is your name, young lady?"

Lydia wiped her eyes with the handkerchief that Mrs. Vermeulen had pressed into her hand and stammered, "Lydia."

"Well, that is a pretty name! What is your last name?"

"Va…Van Arkel!"

When the minister heard her name, he knew for sure. This girl, this blond child with fearful blue eyes, was Esther and John's daughter.

His voice trembled a little as he said, "Is anything too wonderful for the Lord? Even though we are unfaithful, He remains faithful, for He is a Helper and Father of the fatherless!"

Mrs. Vermeulen and Grandma heard these words in amazement. Lydia stopped crying and looked up in surprise when she heard the familiar words from Papa's letter: "A Father of the fatherless."

"Lydia, don't you have a father and mother anymore?"

"No," she replied, shaking her head.

"And your father and mother had an accident in the circus and later died when you were still a little girl?" he continued.

"Yes," she nodded.

"Is she…is she the child of Esther and John?" Mrs. Vermeulen asked in astonishment.

"Yes, she is! I have never gone to her, but the Lord has brought her to me."

Lydia did not understand. What were these people talking about? What was going on? Was she dreaming? How did these people know who she was?

Then the minister began softly to give her a simple explanation of how he knew her parents. Lydia listened to him in amazement, her exhaustion forgotten. She no longer felt so sick and lonely and sad.

When the minister had finished speaking, she said, "The Lord has done it! He can do everything, can't He? He really can do everything."

"Yes, my dear, the Lord can do everything. He promises in His Word that He will care for the fatherless. Oh, we are so rich if we may have the God of Jacob for our Helper."

Grandma, in her corner by the stove, blew her nose, and Mrs. Vermeulen wiped away a few tears. What an amazing evening this had been! Who would have expected something like this to happen?

Now Lydia had to relate to them the whole story of how she had come here. She told her story haltingly and in bits and pieces, but they were able to get a fairly clear idea of what had happened. Lydia would have told them much more, but she had to stop because she was exhausted.

"It's okay, Lydia," the minister said, seeing how tired she was. "We know enough, and you are going to bed now. Don't worry about anything anymore. You are staying with us. The Lord has brought you here; we will not send you away."

Mrs. Vermeulen echoed him, saying, "We most certainly won't!"

******

Three people sat quietly in the cozy living room of the parsonage. The only sounds were the ticking of the clock and an occasional blast of wind howling around the house.

"It has been a strange evening," the minister said, breaking the silence.

His wife and Grandma nodded their heads in agreement.

"Who would have thought this morning that this evening Esther and John van Arkel's daughter would be lying here in our bed?"

They all agreed that none of them would ever have thought this would happen.

"I hope to stop in to see those aunts of hers this week, for there are a few things that must be settled," the minister continued. "Lydia is going to stay here with us, and then I hope we can make up for what that little girl has been missing all these years."

His wife was in complete agreement with him. "I think she is such a sweet girl," she said warmly. "How touching when she said that the Lord has done all this, for He can do everything."

"Yes," Grandma answered, "isn't that a lesson for us as well? It has been Christmas time again, and we have become so accustomed to it! This evening when I saw that child and heard how she was sent away, I thought about another Child who was sent by His Father, who left His Father's house and came to this sinful earth to suffer and to die for the sins of His people. Whether we are young or old, that must become a wonder in our lives. Then the Lord will receive all the honor, for

Thou art, O God, our boast,
the glory of our power;
Thy sovereign grace is e'er
our fortress and our tower.
We lift our heads aloft,
for God, our shield, is o'er us;
Through Him, through Him alone,
whose presence goes before us,
We'll wear the victor's crown,
no more by foes assaulted,
We'll triumph through our King,
by Israel's God exalted.

(Psalter 422:6)

******

Upstairs in the cozy little guest room, Lydia was in a deep, peaceful sleep. Mrs. Vermeulen had helped her get ready for bed, just as if she were her mother, and had snugly tucked a thick blanket around her.

"See, Lydia," she had said, "I'll leave this lamp on, and I'll leave the door open a little bit. If you need anything, just call us, okay?" Her voice had sounded very kind.

Lydia felt very safe here, very secure, but she was too exhausted to answer Mrs. Vermeulen. Her head was reeling from sleepiness, and she longed for some rest.

When Mrs. Vermeulen had tucked her in, she pressed a kiss on Lydia's blond curls and said, "Sleep tight, my child!" To Lydia it had sounded far away, and before Mrs. Vermeulen had left the room, Lydia was in dreamland.

Outside it was cold and dark. Now and then the moon peeked through the clouds, but soon a thick dark cloud covered it again, so it could no longer be seen shining down on the houses and deserted streets.

But, higher, much higher than the moon, the Lord lives, and even though there are such thick dark clouds, He sees and He knows everything. He looks down on everyone.

He heard the cry of a lonely, forsaken girl. Shall He not help those who wait upon Him? Yes, the Lord sees all the trouble and sorrow, and His Word is the Truth. He is "a Father of the fatherless."

Lydia was already in dreamland.

OTHER BOOKS AVAILABLE

BY EARLY FOUNDATIONS PUBLISHERS

Flight from the Enemy by Alien Mol.

"The Germans are coming!" Quickly David motions Rachel and Hannah to hide in the haystack. He has to help Father and Mother! They are in the house. Will they be able to hide in time? Finally the Germans leave. The children hurry back to the house. It is completely silent. They call for Father and Mother, but there is no answer. They are all alone. The girls sobbed. What must David do now? Where must they go now?

ISBN 978-0-9670728-0-7 71 pages paperback 7-10 yrs.

The Mystery of the Necklace by Alie Vogelaar.

Going to a new school often means that you do not immediately have new friends. That was also the case with Paul. And yet there is a classmate who is concerned about the "new boy." John isn't swayed by his classmates and befriends Paul. Sometimes, however, it seems that there is something between him and Paul, and yet it is not only because of the fact that Paul never goes to church. In the school the classmates even whisper that Paul is a thief…

69 pages hardcover 8-12 yrs.

MARGREET SERIES: by Alie Vogelaar.

Not so High, Margreet!	ISBN 978-0-9670728-2-1
What are your Plans, Margreet?	ISBN 978-0-9670728-3-8
At Last… Margreet!	ISBN 978-0-9670728-4-5
I Need Your Help, Margreet!	ISBN 978-0-9670728-5-2
One Day at a Time, Margreet!	ISBN 978-0-9670728-6-9

These books are 120 pages or more hardcover 14-18 yrs.

EDDIE AND LYDIA SERIES: by Alie Vogelaar

A Shot Through the Window	ISBN 978-0-9670728-1-4
No Place to Go	ISBN 978-0-9670728-7-6
Crossroads	ISBN 978-0-9742131-1-8
Falling Towers	ISBN 978-0-9742131-2-5

These books are 100 pages or more   hardcover   10-16 yrs.

The Hasty Promise by Alien Mol

Cherie Mason is fifteen years old and a sophomore in high school. Because of her attitude she at times makes it difficult for herself. But not only because of that, nasty comments are thrown at her. She adores the handicapped Mike in the hospital as well as the adorable daughters of the not so liked teacher Mr. Fayson. For this reason she is called the teacher's pet. When the boys in the class want to take revenge, Cherie is hasty in making a promise. This promise gives her plenty of trouble, especially when her conscience begins to speak. However, she has to keep her promise.

ISBN 978-0-9670728-8-3   110 pages   hardcover   12-16 yrs.

A Great Miracle in a Small Mountain Village by Marian Schalk

This story happened a long time ago, in a small village. That village lies in the middle of the mountains in Germany. The people who lived there are poor. Walter no longer has a father; that is why his mother has to work on a farm. One day something very bad happens. Grief comes into Walter's house. They have to suffer from hunger. Doesn't the Lord take care of them? Yes, a great miracle happens there. The God of Elijah is still alive!

To be read to children from four years old and up. To read by themselves for boys and girls from six years old and up.

ISBN 978-0-9670728-9-0   48 pages   paperback   4-8 yrs.

Shelter From the Storm by Cornelia Klop

Alisha fastens the clasps and puts her autograph book on the picnic table. She skips along with Grandpa to the doghouse. She sees Grandpa's worried look when he checks the dark sky. "You think we'll have an … a …" What was that word again? "A tornado?" she asks with a shiver. "I don't know, but I don't trust it." In the distance they hear rumbling. Left behind on the picnic table lies a blue autograph book, the picture of a bear on its cover…

ISBN 978-0-9742131-0-1 66 pages paperback 4-8 yrs

Jake and Jimmy and the Secret Wishes by Alien Mol

Jake and Jimmy have a secret. Jake wants a rowboat and Jimmy wants a violin. But where will they get them? Mommy and Daddy don't have enough money for a boat or a violin. And so, Jake and Jimmy go on a search of their own and have a lot of adventures along the way.

ISBN 978-0-9742131-3-2 149 pages hardcover 7-12 yrs

The Owl's Nest by W. Schippers

Starting a family in the homestead called the Owl's Nest would be hard enough for Hans Klinge, but his father-in-law's malicious interference and the hatred of his wealthy rival combine to make life most unbearable for Hans. Hans learns that his ways and the ways of God are not the same.

ISBN 978-0-9742131-4-9 138 pages paperback 14 yrs-older

Behind a Closed Door by C.M. DePutter

Sufong lives in Shanghai, a large city in China. Her father owns a restaurant that is well known. But the question remains whether her father will be able to keep his good name since Sufong came in contact with some Christians. Sufong does not dare to speak of this at home until the Lord also becomes most important in the lives of her parents.

ISBN 978-0-9742131-5-6 75 pages hardcover 8-12 yrs

The Torn Children's Bible by C.M. DePutter

This book is the sequel to "Behind a Closed Door." Chi-Pin, Sufong's younger brother, has a plan for the teacher at school. Little does he realize how serious the consequences are for his family and also for the house congregation.

ISBN 978-0-9742131-6-3 107 pages hardcover 8-12 yrs

The Best Prize by S. VanDuinen

When Walter becomes tired of walking Tippy, he thinks of a plan to get rid of the little dog. But when Henry wins first place in a drawing contest, Walter's secret is found out, and Henry learns what the best prize is.

ISBN 978-0-9742131-7-0 39 pages paperback 4-8 yrs

COMING SOON:

A Song in the Inn

EARLY FOUNDATIONS PUBLISHERS
WWW.EFPUBLISHERS.ORG